What is God's Name?

What is God's Name

Darliss Batchelor

Word in Due Season Publishing, LLC

What is God's Name

Darliss Batchelor

Word in Due Season Publishing, LLC
P.O. Box 210541
Auburn Hills, Michigan 48321-0921

Cover Design by Cover Me Book Covers

ISBN 13: 978-0-9829686-1-1

Library of Congress Control Number:2019916555

Printed in the United States of America

Acknowledgements

God is just awesome! I thank Him for gifting me to tell stories and aligning my life such that I can walk in it with ease. I pray my work pleases You.

I must acknowledge my husband, Greg, for allowing me the grace to focus on my writing dreams. I love and respect you for being who you are.

I want to thank the editor for this project, Kiera Northington.

Renee Luke of Cover Me Book Covers. Thank you for pressing through the development of this book's cover!

Last, but not least, I must acknowledge every literary supporter regardless of your contribution to my writing journey. Whether you read any of my books, offered a word of encouragement or recommended my books to others, I appreciate you.

Dedication

I dedicate this book to my father, Arthur Crutchfield, who passed away during the writing of this project.

I named a character after you in your honor.

I miss you!

Chapter 1

Neveah was vibrating with excitement as she went to her closet to retrieve the attire she would wear later in the day. Today was the day she'd waited for her whole life. It was her mother's wedding day and Neveah couldn't wait. Her mother was going to marry a man who Neveah knew made her extremely happy.

She laid the white lace dress, identical to the one her mother would wear, on the bed then returned to the closet for her new shoes that matched her dress perfectly.

A knock on her door, followed by her name being called, drew the teen's attention away from her attire. "Neveah," a voice said from her bedroom door, causing her to look up into the eyes of her mother, the soon-to-be Wyleena Richardson. The glow on the woman's face was undeniable. Neveah couldn't remember a time when her mother looked more radiant.

"I just got back from the hairdresser, so I thought I'd check on you."

"Mama, your hair is gorgeous. Did you do something different with it?"

Wyleena smoothed a stray hair that had escaped from her up-do and said, "I got a new hairstyle. I even let her put a few highlights in. You think Otis will like it?"

"He'll love it."

Wyleena stood in the room for a few beats before speaking. "Well, I'm going to eat a little something, then get ready to go to the chapel. Do you need anything?"

"I think I'm all set, but I could use a bite to eat. I'll come join you for breakfast."

"I would love nothing more." Wyleena stood away from the doorway to allow Neveah to exit. She hugged her tightly and continued, "I know we had some hard times and Lord knows I've spent a lot of lonely nights. But that's all going to change today. This is the beginning of a whole new life for us."

Neveah thought for a moment about all of the times Wyleena had sacrificed to make sure her daughter had nice things. There were also times when though Wyleena thought she hid it; Neveah had heard her mother crying herself to sleep when things didn't work out with a guy she thought was "the one."

"You finally found the man of your dreams and you deserve it. I can't wait," Neveah said as she and her mother headed down the hall toward the kitchen.

***

As Otis and Wyleena pledged their love and devotion to one another, Neveah beamed. The two made a handsome couple. The teen was as excited as, if not more than, her mother. Otis represented more than a husband and provider, he would also be Neveah's father and that meant more to the teen than anything.

During the ceremony, Otis released Wyleena's hand and approached a surprised Neveah. He took her hands in his. Neveah looked into Otis' teary eyes as he cleared his throat before speaking to her.

"Darling, not only do I take your mother in matrimony, but I also take you as well. I know your father passed away when you were a baby, so you don't have a memory of him. You missed out on a lot of things because of his absence. But, I'm here now and I promise you won't miss out anymore. I love you, Neveah, and I'm honored to be your daddy."

Otis took a ring with a small single diamond in it from his pocket and placed it on Neveah's ring finger.

"I want you to always remember that God loves you." He leaned over and kissed her gently on the cheek then returned to a smiling Wyleena's side.

Neveah's eyes watered as she realized her dream had finally come to fruition and she no longer had to be jealous of her friends, who had fathers in their lives. Now, she had one too.

Chapter 2

Otis and Neveah meandered through the mall while Wyleena worked, going in and out of stores buying clothing, shoes, and accessories for Neveah. Otis had followed through on his promise to spoil his new daughter and had taken her on a number of such shopping sprees. However, this trip had added meaning. The duo was looking for the perfect outfit for Neveah to wear to the annual Daddy-Daughter, Mother-Son dance at her school.

The two entered the department store anchoring the mall and headed toward the Junior Department. As Neveah looked through the various racks and displays of clothing, Otis took pictures of her enjoying the experience. Neveah pulled a pair of leggings off the rack and held them up to her waist.

"I think the top I got at the other store would go good with these. What do you think?"

Otis turned his nose up at the long pants. "They're okay. That's for someone older," he said, grabbing a skirt off of the rack. "What about this? I think it'll look great on you."

Neveah surveyed the sliver of fabric masquerading as a skirt. "Um, that's a little short, isn't it?"

"I don't think so. You're young, so you can wear stuff like this. It won't hurt to try it on," he said, laying it over her arm along with the leggings. "I'm sure once you see it on, you'll love it."

Neveah took the items and entered the dressing room after agreeing to try the skirt on, along with the camisole with the thin straps Otis picked out. There was nothing about either piece that excited Neveah, except the sparkles on the top. Otherwise, the outfit was missing a little more fabric than she was comfortable with. She didn't want to disappoint Otis, who seemed to really like the ensemble so she acquiesced.

When she exited the dressing room wearing the skirt and top Otis picked out, she felt naked. Uncovered. Exposed. Otis smiled when he saw her and stood from the chair sitting outside of the fitting room.

"That looks great," he said, pulling his cell phone from his pocket and taking several pictures of Neveah. "Turn around let me get a good look at you."

Neveah did as he asked while he snapped a few more pictures.

"Yeah, I like that," Otis repeated.

Neveah looked at herself in the mirror. Honestly, she wanted to escape back into the dressing room and try on her leggings. Instead, she pretended to consider the outfit out of respect for Otis.

"I'll think about it."

Neveah returned to the dressing room and quickly removed the revealing outfit. After trying on the leggings, she left the dressing room.

"So, what did you decide?" Otis asked.

"I think I'm just going to get the leggings and wear it with the bedazzled t-shirt I got from that other store."

"You can have it all, you know. You don't have to choose one or the other."

"That's okay. I got enough stuff today. I don't even know how I'm going to fit it in my closet as it is."

"We'll just get the skirt, top and leggings. You might change your mind about that other outfit, then you'll already have it."

Chapter 3

"It's your daddy's job to show you how young men are supposed to treat you when they pick you up for a date. Always stay in the car until he comes around to your side and opens the door," Otis said, after opening Neveah's door and holding her hand to help her out.

Neveah nervously stepped out of the vehicle and immediately noticed several people pointing at her and Otis. She could only imagine they were scrutinizing her outfit. Truthfully, she was trying to figure out how she allowed Otis to convince her to wear something that made her so uncomfortable too. She would love to return home and change into her comfy leggings and sparkly shirt, but it was too late for that. They were already running a little late to the dance so she would just have to bear it for one night.

They entered the gymnasium hand-in-hand and though she was a little unnerved, she was ecstatic to finally get to experience what her friends had been speaking of since middle school. She had longed to attend to the Daddy-Daughter, Mother-Son dance and now she had a father to take her.

"Are you hungry?" Otis asked. "They have some food over there on a table."

Neveah looked toward the table and noticed her secret crush, Jaylon Morrison, standing near it. She looked down at her outfit once again and didn't want Jaylon seeing her dressed as she was.

"Maybe I'll have something a little later." Neveah turned her attention away from the food table and toward the dance floor. "Let's dance."

Otis led Neveah to the dance floor just as a slow song began to play. He placed one hand at her waist and held her opposite hand.

"Make sure there's a respectable distance between you and a guy you're slow dancing with," Otis explained, swaying right and left to the beat of the music.

Neveah peeked over Otis' shoulder to see if Jaylon was watching, but couldn't find him. She assumed he must've moved to another part of the gym.

"You like him, don't you?" Otis asked, continuing to move to the rhythm.

"I don't know who you're talking about." Neveah lied, unwilling to tell Otis the truth.

"Neveah Marie, I saw you looking at him when we first came in and again just now."

Neveah dropped her head, embarrassed that Otis had figured her out.

"I guess he's a nice guy," Neveah admitted.

"I don't know why you lied about that. It's okay you like him. He ever try to talk to you?"

"No, I don't think I'm his type."

"Really. What does that mean?"

"I think he likes girls who are more popular."

"You're capable of getting any guy you want. Look at you. You're absolutely gorgeous." Otis delicately ran his hand over Neveah's face. "If I was your age, I'd date you. I'll tell, you what. I'm going to show you what to do to get any man's attention you want."

"You will?"

"Yes but you can't tell your mother, okay? I know your mother wants to keep you sheltered you so she wouldn't understand."

Neveah threw herself into Otis arms. "Thanks Otis! You're the best."

"You're welcome, darling. I'm just doing my job."

Chapter 4

The next night after Wyleena went to work, Neveah heard Otis moving around in the hallway. After a few seconds, she heard a knock at her bedroom door.

"Neveah, are you awake?"

"Yes, come in." Neveah turned on her bedside lamp.

Otis scuffled into the room. "Can I sit on your bed?"

"Sure," Neveah said, making space to accommodate him.

"Remember I told you I was going to teach you how to get any man you want?"

"Yes, I remember."

"Well, tonight is your first lesson. Have you ever kissed a boy?"

Neveah dropped her head, realizing no one had even tried to kiss her before. "No, I haven't."

"I'm going to show you how."

Otis scooted closer to his stepdaughter. He opened his mouth a little and moved his tongue around in demonstration of how to kiss.

"This is what you do. You move your tongues in and out and around each other. Let me see you do it."

Neveah felt awkward, but showed Otis how she would kiss someone based on his instruction.

"That's good. You'll just need some practice but I can help with that too. In fact, let's practice right now."

"I don't know, Otis. I wouldn't feel right kissing you."

"Close your eyes and pretend you're kissing that Jaylon boy. Come on, let's try it."

Otis placed one hand behind Neveah's head and pulled it toward him. His lips pecked hers a few times before he initiated the tongue kiss.

Neveah closed her eyes and followed Otis' lead as their tongues danced with each other. What initially felt awkward to Neveah became pleasant. Just when she relaxed into the kiss, Otis rolled her nipple between his thumb and index finger, causing the seventeen-year-old to jump.

"How does that feel?" he asked, continuing the action. When Neveah didn't respond, he suggested, "Hey, let's try something else and see if you like it."

Otis' hand left Neveah's breast and travelled downward. He pressed his hand into the space where her legs met.

"Open your legs a little bit. You're going to love this."

Reluctantly, Neveah obeyed.

Neveah was conflicted. While what was happening with Otis felt wrong, the sensations coursing through her body as a result felt wonderful.

"You like that?" Otis asked.

Once again, Neveah didn't respond. She wanted to give Otis the right answer, but didn't know what that was so she thought it best not to say anything.

Chapter 5

Several weeks passed where Otis came into Neveah's room a couple of nights a week after Wyleena went to work. Each night, they would kiss while Otis touched Neveah in different parts of her body.

Neveah heard Otis coming down the hall and knew he had a lesson for her that night, so she closed the book she was reading. The formality of him knocking had disappeared weeks ago, so Neveah wasn't surprised when he appeared in her room without warning.

"We've been practicing for quite a while now and I think you're ready for the next lesson."

"If you say so."

"You are. But let's do what we normally do and then I'll tell you what's next."

Otis initiated kissing Neveah, leading them into what had become their normal routine. After a few moments, Otis took Neveah's hand and gently pulled it toward his middle.

"Now, touch me right there."

"No," Neveah said, snatching her hand away. "I'm not doing that."

Otis appeared surprised. "Do you want Jaylon to like you or not?"

"I do, but I'm not doing that to get him. Mama always told me not to do stuff like that."

"Listen here. Your mother is wrong. How do you think she got me? I'm telling you, it's necessary."

Otis had a point. Neveah hadn't thought about her mama doing what Otis was asking her to do.

"I'm trying to help you. Every man you'll ever meet will want you to do certain things and this is one of them. You enjoy it when I touch you here," he said as he teased the most sensitive part of her breasts. "And here," he touched her essence. "Don't you?"

Shyly, Neveah responded, "It's not so bad." Neveah refused to reveal exactly how she felt. Since the beginning of her "training", she'd fought an internal battle between her desire to get and please a boy and how she felt about what she had to do in that effort.

"Relationships are about give and take. No one's going to stay with someone who just takes. You have to give too."

Otis unzipped his pants and fumbled around inside, revealing something that drew a gasp from Neveah

"This is Big Otis. Look at it. It's not scary at all."

Neveah didn't know what to do. She'd never seen one of those before. She heard girls at school talk about them. Some had good things to say about them and others not so good. Since Neveah had no experience, she didn't know where she came down on the subject.

"All you have to do is touch him and give him a little squeeze. He'll wake right up. Go ahead, try it. He won't bite."

Neveah decided to oblige him. *After all, he's helping me and it couldn't hurt to touch his...his...him as he asked.* She reluctantly stretched her hand toward Big Otis. Her hand was just inches from her target when they heard the back door opening, followed by footsteps, Wyleena humming, and the sound of her workbags dropping on the kitchen table as they did every night when she shrugged them off of her shoulder.

Otis hurriedly stood, zipped his pants and left the room, heading toward the kitchen without a word.

"Hey, baby. What are you doing home so early?"

"We were more overstaffed than normal tonight so I volunteered to come home early. What are you doing up? I thought you would be in bed by now."

"I must've known you would be here soon because I was waiting up for you."

More like waiting up for me to touch Big Otis, Neveah thought.

"What did you have in mind?" Wyleena asked, with obvious flirtation in her voice. Neveah could only imagine what Otis was doing to her as she spoke.

"You know Big Otis always has his mind on you and he's already ready for you."

"Well, let's go see exactly what's on his mind tonight."

Neveah heard Wyleena giggling as she and Otis passed her room on the way to their private space.

Chapter 6

After dinner, Wyleena went to work and Neveah washed the dishes, wiped down the appliances and swept the floor. She then settled at the kitchen table to study for a math test while Otis watched television. Neveah silently hoped there wouldn't be another "class" that night. The previous one had gotten a little weird and it was totally useless to her, since she had no intention of going that far in any relationship at that point.

Otis came into the kitchen and stood there. Though she was acutely aware he had entered the space, Neveah pretended she didn't notice him standing there by keeping her head buried in her studies.

Otis cleared his throat, obviously to capture Neveah's attention. She refused to be drawn into interaction with him.

"Look now. I know you see me standing here. We need to start doing your lessons a little earlier. That way, if your mother comes home early again, she won't interrupt us like last time."

Neveah eventually lifted her eyes and gave a visible confirmation she heard him.

"I have a big math test tomorrow and I need the time to study, Otis."

"It sure would be a shame if Jaylon started seeing somebody else, while you're studying for a math test."

Otis' words pricked the young woman's heart. Just that day, Jaylon had finally spoken to her, leaving her wondering if somehow he knew she was preparing herself to show him how she felt about him. Certainly, she didn't want to lose any ground she had gained with him. Neveah figured if she let Otis show her what he wanted, she would have enough time to go over her notes afterward.

"All right."

Neveah rose and headed to her bedroom. She turned on the light and waited on the side of her bed for her stepfather to come in as well.

Otis closed the door securely behind him, unzipped his pants and pulled them as well as his underwear down, revealing a full view of Big Otis.

Neveah's eyes bulged at Otis' lack of modesty. He leaned against the door as he stepped out of each pant and underwear leg. Big Otis didn't appear to need petting or squeezing on this occasion, so Neveah wondered what the lesson could possibly be.

"The other night, you didn't get to know Big Otis. It's very important that you become comfortable with this area of a man's body. You have to know what to do with one of these," he said, physically holding his in his hand.

He found his way to her bed and relaxed himself with his legs gaping open. "Let's start where we were when we were interrupted last time. Go ahead and touch it. It's okay," he said, grasping Neveah's hand and gently guiding it toward Big Otis.

Though she didn't want to, she allowed her hand to be laid on its target. She watched as Otis' eyes closed and his head bent back when she squeezed it. After a few seconds, she jerked her hand away and placed it back in her lap.

"How was that?" he asked, moving his head forward and opening his eyes.

"It was okay." Neveah found the task gross, but knew Otis wouldn't take kindly to hearing that from her.

"I think you're ready for your final exam. You need to let me put him inside you."

Neveah's eyes bulged and her mouth dropped. *Was he suggesting they have sex? How was she going to get out of this? She wasn't ready to have sex with Jaylon, but she never wanted to have sex with Otis!*

"Are you asking me to have sex with you?"

"Jaylon's going to so you might as well let me show you what to do." Otis' smirk was obvious and made Neveah uneasy.

"I appreciate all of your help, but I'm not having sex with anyone until I'm married. Mama and I have talked a lot about this, so I know it's best to wait and that's what I'm going to do," Neveah explained. "I need to get back to studying."

Otis' smirk deepened as he watched Neveah prepare to stand from the bed.

"You obviously don't understand. You're going to do this whether you want to or not."

Otis's smirk swiftly turned into a grimace and he pushed Neveah back on the bed. He leaned over her and pressed his forearm across her throat.

"If you tell anyone about you and me, I will snap your neck. Now you can try me if you want to, but that's a promise."

Neveah cried as Otis began pulling on her pajama bottoms. "Get undressed and you can stop all of that crying." He sat up and removed his hand from her mouth.

"No! Please! I'm a virgin!"

"Well, you won't be in a few minutes. Now get naked. We may not have much time," Otis growled even as he drooled, seeing her naked body revealed to him.

"I've been waiting a long time for this," Otis spewed, putting emphasis on the word, "long."

Neveah broke down as she realized she had spent her last few moments as a virgin. It was obvious there was no convincing Otis. Resigned to her fate and afraid of Otis' response if she tried to get away, she stood before her stepfather completely naked.

"Get over here and lay down. I'm going to take it easy on you tonight, since it's your first time."

Neveah gingerly sat on the bed. Otis violently shoved her down on the mattress with both hands as her sobbing intensified.

Otis smiled as he crawled on top of her.

"That's a good girl. Remember, God loves you and so do I."

Chapter 7

Neveah and Wyleena went into the school together for one of the final parent/teacher conferences of Neveah's high school career. Wyleena was chattering about how proud she was of her daughter's academic accomplishments and the bright future she had as a result, but Neveah's mind was somewhere else.

Wyleena stopped talking and observed Neveah. She patted her on the arm. "Hey, you're awfully quiet lately. Is everything okay?"

Neveah returned her mother's glance. She didn't want to lie, but she wasn't sure if she should tell the truth either.

"Maybe I'm just a little nervous about what I'll do once I graduate."

"The plan is for you to go to college."

"I know, Mama, but what if I can't get in? What will I do then?"

"You never seemed concerned before. Why are you concerned now?"

"I don't know, Mama. I guess I'm a little scared. That's all." Neveah wanted to reveal her true concern, but couldn't bring herself to do so. Her mother would find out about that soon enough.

Wyleena stopped walking and gently cupped Neveah's chin in her hand. "Listen, baby. I know you're going into a whole new phase in your life and that can be a little scary, but you're going to be just fine. Don't worry. Otis and I have your back, okay?"

Neveah nodded her head as they headed into Mrs. Roger's classroom to discuss how she was doing in her Honors Pre-Calculus class.

"Hello, Neveah. Hi, Mrs. Richardson. It's nice to see you again," Mrs. Rogers said as she and Wyleena shook hands. "Come on in and let's chat a bit."

Neveah took a seat next to her mother and waited for Mrs. Rogers to go over her progress. The teacher pulled up Neveah's information on the laptop sitting on her desk and looked over her glasses at Neveah.

"Here's Neveah's grade so far in my class," Mrs. Rogers turned the screen toward Wyleena, who shook her head in response.

"This can't be Neveah's grade. She's an Honor Roll student and math has always been her strong point."

"I was shocked, too. Neveah's performance hasn't been good this year, yet she's been one of my best students the entire time she's been in high school. The question is what's changed?"

Wyleena faced her daughter. "What is going on, Neveah? This isn't like you. Is the work too hard for you?"

Neveah shrugged her shoulders though she knew the work wasn't the problem. The issue was Otis' visits to her room were becoming more often and more demanding as well.

"This is the response I got when I asked her why she's not doing well in this class. I also noticed Neveah daydreaming, missing assignments and she even fell asleep a couple of times in class. I'm concerned Neveah is relaxing because this is her senior year and she's not in danger of missing graduation."

Wyleena peered at Neveah as she stood, "Don't worry. Neveah will get this grade up." She turned her gaze to Mrs. Rogers and shook her hand. "Thank you for bringing this to my attention."

Wyleena silently moved through Neveah's entire schedule with the same outcome. Neveah wasn't doing well academically. When the two entered the vehicle and prepared to leave, Wyleena faced her daughter. "Now I understand why you're concerned about getting into college all of a sudden. I don't know what's going on, but you need to start talking because this is completely unacceptable."

"Mama, I promise I'm going to get my grades up. Don't worry."

"I certainly hope so."

Neveah hated to disappoint her mother and she knew her poor grades were causing her to feel that way. Telling her mother her new husband was sexually abusing her on a regular basis would cause even greater devastation. What was Neveah to do?

CHAPTER 8

"Leave me alone!" Neveah screamed. "I don't want to do this!"

Tears streamed down her face as begged her assailant to leave her alone. She wrestled with him, attempting to free herself from his grasp.

"Please stop," she continued, her screaming giving way to sobbing. "I'm begging you. Please don't do this."

Hands touched her, causing her to yell, "Why won't you stop?"

"Remember, God loves you and so do I," the voice said as it always did after the event.

The shaking caused Neveah to awaken. Noticing the figure standing next to her bed, she pushed herself away with her feet, forced all of her bed coverings into a pile, and cowered in the corner against the wall, her head on her bent knees.

"Neveah, wake up," Wyleena said, sitting on the bed, attempting to pull her daughter close to her. "You're shaking. Everything's okay. It was only a nightmare."

Neveah lifted her head, realizing she wasn't in any danger. She scooted next to her mother who pulled her close. The reality of the nightmare shook her to her core.

"What is going on?" Wyleena asked. "You were screaming." Wyleena gently rocked her daughter.

Neveah wiped the moisture that gathered on her face. "Everything is fine."

"Don't tell me everything is okay when I can see it's not. Talk to me."

 As Neveah continued to gather herself, she looked up at her mother and wondered if she should tell her. *Would her mother believe her if she told her? How would her mother feel after hearing what she had to say?*

***

The next morning, Neveah and her mother were in the kitchen while Wyleena prepared breakfast. The incident from the day before seemed to have been forgotten. But Neveah had been up thinking about her dilemma most of the night.

"Are you ready to talk about it?"

"Ready to talk about what?" Neveah knew exactly what her mother wanted to discuss. The question was if Neveah was ready.

"I'm talking about your episode yesterday."

Neveah hesitated, attempting to decide what to do. Her mother seemed sincerely interested in what her daughter was going through, so perhaps it would be a good time for Neveah to explain again.

"Mama, Otis makes me have sex with him all the time and you don't want to know what else he does."

Wyleena looked at her daughter and said, "Is that what you're trying to tell me that episode was about?"

"It's true. I wouldn't lie to you about something like this."

"Girl, I don't know what he needs with you, when he's got a real woman like me," Wyleena said as she cupped her voluminous breasts and pushed them up.

"Well, he does."

"There is no way."

"Why won't you believe me?"

Otis shuffled into the kitchen as his wife, Wyleena, prepared breakfast. He kissed her, allowing his lips to linger a little longer for emphasis, then smacked her on her bottom which jiggled in response. He pulled out the chair at the head of the table and sat. Eyeing the young woman sitting next to him, Otis ran his tongue over his lips and smiled, revealing a couple of missing teeth.

"Good morning, little girl."

"Morning."

"How did you sleep?" he joked.

"Not well. I had another nightmare."

Otis leaned over to lay hands on his stepdaughter. "Let me pray for you. We might be able to get rid of these nightmares." He laughed heartily.

Neveah moved out of his reach. "No, don't touch me," she warned. "Don't ever put your hands on me."

Wyleena turned toward her daughter. "Neveah, I'm not going to stand here and let you disrespect this man."

"You living in my house and I'll touch you whenever I want," Otis said, allowing his tongue to play in the gap left by his missing front teeth.

"It's interesting you would say that, Otis. My child has been telling me you've been playing around with her."

"What do you mean?" He nervously glanced at Neveah.

"You know what I mean. She says you're having sex with her."

"Now, you know I ain't had sex with no one but you, Wyleena. I don't know what would make her lie on me like that."

"Mama! Why are you telling him what I told you?"

"If you didn't want me to say anything, you shouldn't have told me."

"We need to do something about this child lying," Otis explained, wagging his finger at Neveah.

"Lying?" Neveah couldn't believe he would call her a liar.

"Yeah, lying. Trying to come between me and your mama," Otis responded, approaching his wife from behind as she stood at the stove. "Wyleena, I took this child in and treated her like she was my own since she didn't have a daddy. Why would I do something like that to her, huh? Besides, when a man has a woman like you, he doesn't need a child." Otis winked at Neveah as he hugged his wife.

Otis lavished his attention on Wyleena, affirming his love only for her. Wyleena turned around and hugged her husband who responded by kissing her on the neck, causing her to release a sound which sounded like a kitten purring to Neveah.

"You two should get a room," Neveah suggested, gagging at the scene before her. If her mother only knew the truth, she wouldn't respond to Otis like that.

Wyleena opened her eyes and shot a look at her daughter. "I don't want to hear another word about Otis having sex with you. Do you understand?"

"But, Mama!" Neveah pleaded. If she couldn't tell her mother, who could she tell?

"I mean it. Now, Otis has been good to you. He made sure you had everything you needed and more. It's time you respect him for being the man of the house."

Neveah realized there was no way she could win this battle. Her mother was too enamored with Otis to even entertain the possibility of wrongdoing on his part.

"Come on, baby! I got a special treat for you," Wyleena said as she sashayed toward the master bedroom.

"Mercy," he responded, following behind his wife. He smiled at Neveah, revealing every tooth that was left in his mouth. Neveah rolled her eyes. Something had to give because Otis showed absolutely no sign of letting up.

CHAPTER 9

Neveah laid in bed with tears in her eyes, fearing a repeat of the long-established pattern. She closed her eyes and hoped Otis would fall asleep, get sick or something so he couldn't do this anymore.

Neveah tried numerous times to inform Wyleena about what was going on, but her mother just couldn't see her loving and supportive husband doing what Neveah said he did.

Hearing the shuffle of house shoes sliding across the wood floors in the hall indicated her wish wouldn't be granted, at least not tonight. *Maybe he's going to the bathroom*, she thought hopefully. But, the creaking of her bedroom door diminished all hope of a rescue once again.

"Are you awake?" he asked huskily.

She refused to answer. It might help if he thought she wasn't aware of his presence, though it had never worked before.

"I know you hear me. I can tell by your breathing you're not sleep."

She once again chose to maintain her silence, hoping it might change the typical course of things. She heard the sound of the zipper on his jeans and knew there would be no reprieve. The pants hit the floor and she heard the sound of his feet landing as each of them stepped out of the pant legs. Desiring to make things go as quickly as possible, she threw the covers off, pulled down her sleep pants and got into position.

"Little girl, you sure know how to turn me on. Your mama never made me feel the way you do. You do what I like and that sure makes me happy. Since you make me feel good, I'm going to make you feel good, too."

He crawled into the twin-size bed and positioned himself behind her. He ran his hand tenderly over her bare bottom. His action caused her to squirm.

"Where do you want me to put it? It's your choice tonight."

Back in your pants, she thought.

"I feel like I can go a while, so we'll just do both. If you satisfy me, I'm going to do something I don't even do for your mama," Otis said, gripping Neveah's waist.

Neveah knew exactly what that meant. She'd experienced it before and didn't find it all that enjoyable. She had tired of the routine a long time ago, but didn't see an alternative to cooperating...or was there? A thought presented itself and for the first time she considered doing something different. Instinct kicked in and she realized there was no requirement to respond to Otis as she normally would. If he followed through on his threats, so be it.

"Remember, God loves you and so do I." Otis repeated this sentiment every time he came into her room for this purpose.

Neveah felt his member preparing to enter her. Instead of accepting what was to come, she made a split-second decision. Since her mother didn't believe her and there was no one else to help, she realized she needed to handle the situation herself. She got off of her knees, rolled onto her back and pummeled her stepfather with her fists, feet and anything else she could think of to disturb his plan.

Otis laid on top of Neveah and pinned her wrists to the bed, stopping the punches. Neveah continued struggling against the much bigger and stronger man, determined to give it everything she could.

"Why are you fighting me?" he grunted, tussling with his stepdaughter.

"I'm not going to let you keep doing this to me," Neveah said through gritted teeth.

Otis moved to reposition himself, providing Neveah leverage to push him off of her. When he fell to the floor, she ran toward the bedroom door. Otis grabbed her ankles, taking them out from under her and causing her to fall face-first onto the floor.

"Where are you going?" Otis asked, pulling Neveah toward him. "Oh, I get it. You want to play a game? I'm good with that."

"No, I want you to leave me alone. I'm not going to let you keep doing what you've been doing to me. I'm telling Mama." Neveah clawed the wood floor, trying to get away from Otis.

Otis laughed heartily. "That's funny. You already told your mama and she didn't believe you. Why do you think she's going to believe you now? You might as well get back on that bed and do what you're told, because I'm not leaving this room until I get what I came in here for."

The door swung open, slamming into the wall behind it and Wyleena appeared, wielding a butcher knife and a pot that had steam rising from it. She looked at her husband's state of undress.

"So, it's true?" Wyleena asked, stepping forward into the room. "You have been raping my daughter."

"No, baby. I told you that's not true," Otis responded, pulling his pants up and trying to stuff Big Otis back into them.

"Oh, really?"

"Like I told you before, I would never do anything like that to Neveah. She's my daughter."

"Is that so? How do you explain you standing there with Big Otis at attention and my daughter with her sleep pants down?"

Otis struggled to find an answer to Wyleena's question as she patiently waited. Neveah stood and pulled up her pants, thankful her mother finally witnessed what was happening.

"Where do you want me to put it?" Wyleena asked.

"Put what?" Otis' voice quivered as he backed away from his wife.

"Let's try this one. If you satisfy me, I'm going to do something for you I don't even do for your mama."

"Baby, what's going on?"

Wyleena stalked Otis. "You never answered my first question. Where do you want me to put it?"

"What are you planning on doing with that knife and whatever is in that pot?"

"As soon as you tell me where you want me to put it, I'm going to put them there. The grits first to slow you down so I can get to work with the knife."

Otis rushed the door, attempting to escape from the tight quarters. Holding his pants up, he went right and Wyleena met him there. He went left, she met him there, too. He faked right, giving himself time to exit the room, since heavy-set Wyleena couldn't regroup fast enough to catch him. He escaped the bedroom and ran into the living room with his wife directly behind him.

Neveah heard the unmistakable sound of the pot colliding with a wall, immediately followed by Otis' screams.

"What's the matter? Did I give it to you wrong?"

Otis continued screaming from the assault of the steaming hot grits.

Wyleena straddled her husband and wrestled with him.

"No, Wyleena. Why are you trying to pull my pants down? What are you trying to do?" Otis yelled as he wrestled with his wife, trying to keep his pants up. "I don't understand what's going on!"

"Well, you're gonna learn today!"

"Just let me go. I'll leave right now."

"Oh, you're gonna leave. I can guarantee that." Wyleena managed to gain control of Otis' pants as he continued to swipe at the grits that were burning his skin. She pulled his pants down a bit and released Big Otis from his home. She grabbed the cleaver and positioned it over her target. Neveah turned her head away, anticipating what was about to happen as Otis continued to beg. She heard the knife hit the floor and knew Big Otis had been freed from its owner.

As Otis screeched in pain, grabbing the place where Big Otis used to live, Wyleena continued sitting on him with a blank stare on her face.

"Help me," he begged.

As blood poured onto the floor, Otis cried. His breath became shallower until finally it stopped and Otis closed his eyes.

Wyleena slowly rose from Otis' still body and kicked him once she stood. She approached her daughter who was standing with her back toward her mother.

"I'm so sorry I didn't believe you. Are you okay?" Wyleena asked.

Neveah turned toward her mother and ran into her arms. Wyleena held her distraught daughter close and kissed her on the forehead.

Neveah nodded. "Yes, I'm okay. How did you know what was happening tonight?"

"I came home from work early and while I was fixing myself some grits, I heard a scuffle. That's when I came to your room armed to deal with an intruder and found Otis in here."

"Shouldn't we call for help?"

"We are not calling for help. He wasn't thinking about help when he was raping you. We're just going to let him lay there and die, if he isn't already dead. Once the police get involved, I'm either going to end up dead or in jail behind this and I don't want you to be around for that. Go get Otis' wallet."

Neveah ran to the bedroom and grabbed Otis' wallet from the top of the dresser.

"Otis just got paid. He always cashes his check as soon as he gets it, so there should be plenty of money in there."

Wyleena opened the wallet and removed the bills, then pressed them into Neveah's hand.

"Take this money and leave the city."

"I don't want to leave you." Neveah began to hyperventilate. "I can't breathe!"

"This is no time to have for you to be falling apart. Pull it together and focus."

"Okay." Neveah obeyed and began to whimper.

"I want you to leave here. You're going to have to make your own way, but I believe you can do it."

"Where am I going to go? I can't just wander the streets."

"Make your way to Louisville, Kentucky."

"Who lives in Louisville?"

"Your aunt."

"What aunt?"

"Monique. She's your father's sister."

"Auntie Monique is really my aunt? I thought she was just your best friend!"

"While I'm telling secrets, your father is alive too."

"You told me he was dead!"

"He's strung out bad, baby, and I didn't want you to go looking for him. I let Monique see you to satisfy your daddy so he wouldn't try to see you."

Wyleena fumbled with the pocket of her pants and pulled out her cell phone. "Here's my cell phone. I won't be needing it. I just loaded it up with minutes, so it should last you for a while. Monique's number is in there. Call her. Maybe you can live with her."

"Please, Mama, don't make me leave."

"We don't have much time. Be strong, Neveah. You can handle this. Catch a bus or a train, whichever is cheaper, and make a new life. No matter what happens, remember I love you and I did this for you. Now, get you some clothes and some of your favorite things, throw them in as many bags as you can carry and go."

***

Neveah looked out of the window of the moving bus. Leaving the city where she was born and raised caused her a great deal of angst. More than that, she was worried about her mother. Not knowing what would happen to her was wearing Neveah out emotionally. Wyleena made it abundantly clear she wanted her to get as far away from the area as possible in order to allow her to escape the drama which was to unfold.

Suddenly, the bus slowed just north of the Michigan-Ohio border and pulled to the side of the road. Neveah noticed the lights from the state police vehicles and wondered, along with the rest of the passengers, what was happening. After a few moments, police officers climbed onto the bus. One of them appeared to be looking from his cell phone to the faces of those on the bus. The other one stood near the front of the bus. The officer got to her row and she unsuccessfully attempted to hide by pulling her hat down on her head and looking away from the officer.

"Neveah Miller?"

Neveah didn't respond. If she didn't respond maybe he might think he had the wrong person. Neveah wasn't sure why the police were looking for her and she didn't want to know. Her focus was on getting to Kentucky where Aunt Monique lived, hoping she would be willing to take her in.

"Ma'am, can you gather your things and exit the bus with us?"

"Why, sir? What did I do?"

"Please get your belongings and come with us."

Neveah exited the bus with the authorities. They ushered her to a squad car and placed her in the backseat.

"I'm Officer Torres. Are you Neveah Miller?" one of the officers asked through the grate separating the backseat from the front.

"Yes, sir. What is this all about?"

"Do you know someone named Wyleena Richardson?"

"Yes, sir. That's my mama. Did something happen to her?" Neveah panicked.

"Something happened to Otis Richardson."

"What happened to him?"

"Someone killed him. You don't know anything about that, do you?"

"No, sir, I don't."

"You don't seem too broken up about it. He did live in the house with you and your mother, right?"

"Yes. He wasn't a nice man though, so he probably got what he deserved."

"Why would you say that?"

"I'd rather not talk about it, if it's okay with you." Neveah looked out of the window of the moving police squad car.

"Did you kill him?"

"No, sir. Even though he was mean to me, I wouldn't be able to kill him."

"What about your mother? Did she get along okay with Otis?"

"They got along most of the time. They always tried to keep me out of their problems, so I don't know what was going on in their relationship. Where are you taking me?"

"I have to take you to the police station. We've been looking for you since we discovered what happened to Otis. His brother mentioned you, so we've been looking for you. We had to make sure you weren't hurt as well. Now that we've found you, we have to get you all squared away with a home."

"I can take care of myself."

"I'm afraid we can't allow that. You're too young. By the way, why were you on that bus heading out of town?"

"Otis was doing bad things to me and I didn't see another way to make it stop. So, I left."

"Did your mother know Otis did bad things to you?"

"I don't know. It didn't matter. I had to get out of there."

"Okay. I guess you can enjoy the rest of the ride."

***

Neveah followed the officer into a room with a table and a few chairs.

"Have a seat here, young lady."

Neveah sat in a chair and placed her bags beside her on the grimy gray floor. She turned her attention to the police officer, waiting to see what would happen next.

"Are you hungry? Want something to drink?" the officer asked, removing the jacket he wore and placing it on the back of a chair opposite Neveah.

"No, thank you."

"I'm sure you're a little scared and it's a little uncomfortable right now, but we're trying to do the right thing by you."

Neveah chose not to respond to the officer since she wasn't sure what he was really trying to do. She watched too many TV shows where police officers managed to make people feel comfortable, only to get them to say something that would incriminate them. She wasn't going to say anything that might cause trouble for her or her mother if she could help it. She wondered if she'd already said too much on the ride over. That was water under the bridge though and she wouldn't volunteer any more information.

"Where's my mother? You said something happened to Otis, but you didn't mention if my mother is okay." Neveah figured there wouldn't be any harm in asking about her mother.

The officer studied Neveah for what seemed like minutes, causing Neveah to shift in her seat.

Finally, he broke his silence. "I don't know. We were concerned about your safety, considering the scene at your home."

"Would it be disrespectful to say I don't believe you when you say you don't know where my mother is?"

"Why don't you believe me?"

"I just get the feeling you know but don't want to tell me. The question is why you're holding back."

"All right. I heard some information, but it didn't come from an official source and I don't want to tell you something that's not true, okay?"

Neveah dropped her head onto the table and released the emotions she'd been dealing with all morning. The shock of witnessing her mother kill Otis, being sent away and finding herself on a bus, headed to a new life alone without her mother there to support her all caused her deep anxiety. She allowed the tears and sobs she'd been holding in to escape.

The officer left the room and returned with a female officer who came to Neveah's side. "Oh, honey. It's okay," she said, comforting the young woman. She took a few tissues from a box on the table and stuffed them into Neveah's hand. Neveah took them and cleaned her face and nose.

"My mama's dead, isn't she? That's why you won't tell me what happened," Neveah said, seeking a response from the male officer.

"I told you I'm not sure."

The female officer rocked Neveah in her arms as she began to bawl once again. Neveah realized she was really all alone in this world, except for her aunt who she thought was her mother's friend, and her father who she never met.

"We're focused on you right now. We need to get you someplace you can be cared for. You're going to a good foster home soon. I can personally vouch for this woman. She is a loving person who takes really good care of the children sent to her. You'll love her."

Neveah realized these people were not going to tell her about her mother one way or the other. She would just have to make it a point to keep asking until someone told her the truth. Until then, she had to be concerned about her own well-being and since she was a minor, she had to do what they decided for her. She would cooperate and go to the foster home. It had to be better than trying to figure out what to do on her own.

CHAPTER 10

Neveah and the female officer arrived in front of a huge home with plenty of flowers in the well-manicured yard and more in pots sitting on the front porch. The circular driveway held a couple of large SUVs as well as a sports car. A look at the other homes on the street convinced Neveah that she was in a well-off area. As she stepped out of the car and grabbed her bag, the front door of the home opened and a woman stepped out wearing a pink muu-muu dress that covered her well-endowed body.

"Hi there! I'm Bethany Morris. You must be Neveah!"

Neveah watched as the woman quickly approached with open arms. She believed the woman intended to hug her, but she wasn't comfortable with that. After all, she had just left home earlier in the day and now she would be living with this woman she didn't know and whoever else lived in the home. When the woman reached for her, Neveah pulled away.

The woman appeared surprised. "I understand and I won't push you. Just know you are in a safe place." She looked at Neveah closely. "You are a beautiful young lady and God loves you. I want you to know that."

Neveah broke down crying once again. *How could God love her with all that had happened to her? Did God even exist?*

"Oh honey," the woman said, finally wrapping her arms around her. Neveah fell into the comfort of the woman. Her body's softness reminded Neveah of her mother. "You're going to be fine. I heard about your circumstances, so I know it's tough. But don't worry, I'm going to take really good care of you."

"Neveah," the officer said, "I'm going to go now. You're in good hands."

"Thank you."

"Good luck to you," the woman said as she entered the police car before pulling away from the curb.

Neveah turned her attention back to her foster mother, waiting for her to tell her what to do next.

"So, let's get your things upstairs to your room. You're the only girl, so you'll have your own space."

Neveah picked up her belongings and followed the woman into the house. Once inside, she viewed the plush furnishings of the home. The tall ceiling hosted a glass chandelier the likes of which Neveah had never seen before. The cream-colored furniture sitting on deep wood floors belied the fact young people lived there. Moving through what seemed to be the great room, the kitchen came into view. Neveah took this room in and thought it looked brand new. The eyes of the stove were spotless, there were no dirty dishes in the sink and there wasn't even the smallest crumb on the floor or countertop.

"Feel free to make yourself at home here in the kitchen. If it's in the refrigerator or cabinets, you can have it. Just make sure you clean up after yourself. That's the only rule."

The pair went up the staircase leading to the bedrooms.

"Your bedroom is at the end of the hall," Bethany said, leading Neveah past three huge bedrooms and a bathroom. Finally, they entered a room with yellow walls, wood floors, pink and yellow patterned rugs and a white queen size bed. "This is your own personal space. There's even a bathroom in here. Do you like it?"

"I've never had a room like this," Neveah said, turning in a circle viewing every angle of the room. "It's beautiful."

"I'm glad you like it. I'll leave you for a little while so you can get settled in. If you need anything, just holler. When you're ready, come on downstairs. I'll be cooking dinner shortly and maybe you'd like to help."

"Okay, thank you for everything."

Bethany left the room and Neveah fell onto the bed. Even the mattress was soft and bouncy. Her mattress at home didn't have any bounce left. She stood and went to the attached bathroom and, for the first time that day, she smiled. She was worried about her mother and she hated what happened to Otis, but she smiled anyway. She realized for the first time in a long time she could relax and not have to worry about dealing with Otis. She decided to put her things away and lay in the bed for a little bit. She would call her aunt Monique later to let her know what happened.

***

"Neveah. Are you okay?" Neveah sat straight up in the bed after hearing her name called, accompanied by knocking on the bedroom door. She looked around the unfamiliar space and was reminded that she was no longer at home. She was in her new home.

"Yes, I'm okay. I just fell asleep." Neveah threw her legs over the side of the bed and rubbed her eyes.

"Come on down for dinner. The rest of the family is waiting to meet you," Bethany said.

"Give me a second to freshen up and I'll be there."

"Okay, you should have everything you need. If there's something missing, let me know."

Neveah heard the woman walk away, so she went to the bathroom to wash her face and hands for dinner. She passed a full-length mirror and looked at herself for a moment. Her life had changed in one day and there was still potential for more change considering she was living in a home with complete strangers. She looked tired so she was looking forward to crawling back in bed after dinner and spending a little time with the others.

Neveah followed the voices as she walked through the kitchen toward the dining room. She stepped into the room, causing all talking to cease. She noticed four young men who appeared to be around her age, sitting at the table staring at her. Their startled expressions told Neveah they were expecting someone different. Her first thought was to check her clothing. Once she realized everything was as it should be, she wondered if it was because they thought she was homely or if it was because she was the only black person in the house.

Bethany stood and gestured toward an empty seat at the large table, "Come on and have a seat."

Initially, Neveah hesitated before moving around to the opposite side of the table between two of the young men who each scooted their seats away from hers.

"Paul, what did I teach you about how to treat a young lady?"

Paul slowly stood and pulled out Neveah's seat. She sat after saying, "Thank you."

The foster care mother introduced Paul, Sean, Collin, and Josh before saying grace and dishing up food from the bowls and platters on the table.

"So, I take it your room is acceptable since you were comfortable enough to take a long nap."

"It's perfect."

"I guess it is perfect since she gets a room by herself," Collin said.

"She can't room with you guys, so what do you expect?" Miss Bethany pointed out.

"Well, it's not fair we have to share and she doesn't."

"We are not having this discussion again. This is the way it is so accept it and move on."

The room fell silent again as Neveah looked around the table at the others sitting there. Everyone had their head down except Collin, who stared at her, not shifting his eyes even when he noticed her looking at him. The intensity in his gaze felt like hatred though Neveah wondered why, considering this was the first time she'd ever seen him. She wondered if he would be a problem for her there. It certainly seemed possible but Neveah hoped he wouldn't.

CHAPTER 11

Neveah sat on the side of the bed and looked through the bags she packed before leaving home. She pulled a few pictures out and viewed them. One was of her and her mother just a few short weeks ago. She remembered the occasion of the picture, too. It was her mother's birthday. A few tears streamed down her cheeks as concerns about her mother arose. There were also various images of other family members as well. Neveah placed those back in her bag and continued looking for her phone. She finally found it and searched for Auntie Monique's number. Once she found it, she pressed "call" and the phone rang.

"Hey, Wyleena. I'm at work so I can only talk for a minute. What's going on?"

"Hi, Auntie Monique. It's Neveah."

"Hey! Is everything okay?"

"No, it's not."

"What's wrong?"

"I'm in a foster home."

"Foster home? Where's Wyleena?"

"I don't know where Mama is. Otis is dead and Mama did it. She sent me away because she didn't want me to have to deal with whatever happened."

"Oh, my goodness! I told Wyleena to leave that man a long time ago. He's a cheater and he didn't always treat your mother right."

"I didn't know about all of that, but that's not why she killed him, though."

"Why else would she kill Otis?"

"She found out he was making me have sex with him."

Monique went silent for so long Neveah though they had lost the connection. Her phone's screen indicated the call was still in effect.

"Hello?"

"I'm here. I'm just shocked."

"Why didn't tell me you were my real aunt?"

"Who told you that?"

"Mama told me before I left the house. She told me my daddy was alive, too. Is that true?"

Once again, Neveah had to check her phone to insure the connection was still intact.

Finally, Monique broke the silence, "It's true. Your dad is my brother. I don't know where he is but as far as I know, he's still alive. I don't hear from him much but he reaches out every now and then."

"Why didn't I ever meet him? He doesn't love me? Is that why I never knew anything about him?"

"Your father has a drug problem, so he hasn't been stable for a very long time. He just couldn't get himself together enough to be a good father to you, so he felt you would be better off without him."

"Oh."

"I've always shared pictures and news about you with him over the years and he was extremely proud of you. He regrets not being there but he loves you."

Neveah sniffled as she grieved all the years lost with her father. "That's good to know. When you talk to him again, will you give him this number? I think I need that connection with him, especially now with Mama not being around."

"I don't know when I'll talk to Aaron again, but I will give him your number. Make sure you call me if you need anything."

"Auntie Monique, that's another reason I called. Can I come live with you? I mean, my foster mother is nice and all, but she's not family."

"Honey, I don't know if that would work out. I'm not really set up for kids."

"I'm not a kid. I'm seventeen. You don't need to do much for me. All I need is a place to stay and food to eat."

"I'm going to be completely honest with you. I have a boyfriend, Neveah, and I don't know if I can trust you around him. I don't know what happened between you and Otis and how that all came about, but I don't want anything like that going on here."

"You think I might go after your boyfriend?"

"I don't know. Why else would Otis look to you for sex when he had your mother and...?"

"You actually believe I wanted to have sex with Otis?"

"It's not impossible."

Neveah was appalled that her aunt, someone who had known her since she was a baby, would suggest that not only was she responsible for the abuse she had endured from Otis, but also would assume Neveah would go after her boyfriend.

"Before I hang up, I just want you to know Otis started coming in my room at night not long after him and Mama got married. I didn't even know what sex was before he showed up. As far as your boyfriend, I've never even met him. I'm really disappointed that you think so little of me."

"I'll help you however I can, but you can't come live with me."

"Bye." Neveah ended the call with her aunt.

The idea that Monique was her aunt and her father was still alive would take some getting used to. At least she wasn't alone in the world any longer. She sincerely hoped she would get a chance to talk to her father. Maybe, he had his life together enough to take her in. Miss Bethany was nice and all, but she was a stranger. Neveah craved a strong family connection more than anything.

CHAPTER 12

"This is how you make cheesecake," Bethany said as she and Neveah worked on the creation.

Neveah had enjoyed the time she'd spent with her foster family. Sure, some of her interaction with the foster brothers had been challenging, especially with Collin who seemed to have an issue with Neveah she didn't understand.

Her new school was even great. She'd made new friends and was learning new things, including how to speak Spanish. If she continued to do well, she was on track to graduate early if she chose.

"Do you like cherry or strawberry topping?" Bethany asked, holding the container of strawberry topping in one hand and cherry topping in the other.

"It doesn't make a difference to me but if I had to pick, I would choose strawberry."

"I want cherry," a deep voice came from behind them, causing Bethany and Neveah to turn to the source.

"Too late. I asked Neveah and she chose. We'll do cherry next time," Bethany said as she placed the cherry topping back in the cabinet.

"But I want cherry. Why does Neveah always get her way?"

"She was in here helping me prepare dinner for everyone, while you were upstairs playing video games and watching television. When you start doing some of that, you can choose. Should I put you on the schedule for dinner this week?"

Collin's face turned red. Neveah could've sworn she saw smoke coming from his ears as he stomped out of the kitchen and up the stairs.

"Miss Bethany, why don't we just do cherry? It really doesn't matter to me and it seems important to Collin."

"I know you're just doing that because it's what Collin wants, but I'm not going to give in. If I do, he'll manipulate the situation all of the time to get his way and I'm not going to tolerate that."

"Can I ask you something?"

"Certainly."

"Why doesn't Collin like me? I mean, he doesn't have to love me, I just wish he would be cordial."

"Collin is angry in general. He's gone through a lot of hard circumstances and it's made him bitter. He thinks people owe him because of that. He doesn't understand that none of us were responsible for what he experienced. He shouldn't be taking it out on you for sure."

"I thought it was personal but maybe it's not."

"Don't take it personally. He's been like that with everybody here at one time or another. I'll talk to him again. He just needs a reminder that he needs to check his behavior. I don't want him upsetting you. You've been through enough."

CHAPTER 13

Neveah typed her mother's name into the Internet search engine to see if she could find out what happened to her. She held her breath as she clicked on the "search" button and waited to see what came up. Several articles were listed about Otis' murder, so she clicked on the first one to see what it revealed. She skimmed over the paragraphs, trying to get to the information she was looking for. While her mother was listed as a suspect, there was no information about whether she'd been located. Instead the article focused on Otis and the murder. She looked at the date of the article and realized it had been written the same day the murder happened. Her mother could've been found and killed since then.

Neveah made a decision she hoped would lead her to the answer she was looking for. She had to at least try to find out the truth. Not knowing kept her up at night. Her mother had warned her she might be killed as a result of what happened and that's what laid heavily on Neveah's heart the most.

She decided to contact Otis' sister to express her condolences and ask about her mother. The woman adored Neveah under normal circumstances but these circumstances were anything but normal. She acknowledged the fact the woman might not want to talk to her but Neveah just had to try. She looked through the phone's contacts to see if her number was there and found it. Pressing the contact information, hearing the phone ringing and waiting for the call to be answered, caused Neveah a bit of anxiety. But, her desire to know the truth outweighed her fear.

"I'm assuming this is Neveah calling me from this number, but I have no desire to talk to you. I'll be blocking this number as soon as I hang up." The call disconnected before Neveah could even announce herself. She waited a few moments, trying to decide if she should try again. Eventually, she chose to leave the woman alone since she knew who was calling and indicated she would block the number, anyway. Neveah needed another plan.

Her next idea was to contact Miss Nancy, their elderly neighbor who was loving yet nosy. If anyone knew what happened on that block, it would be her. She looked her up and called her. *Why hadn't she thought to contact her in the first place?*

"Hello," Miss Nancy's voice cracked.

"Miss Nancy, this is Neveah. Do you remember me?"

"Baby, where are you? I've been worried about you."

"I'm in a foster home."

"Oh, dear. Are you okay?"

"I'm fine, Miss Nancy."

"It sure is a shame what happened over at your house. The whole street was full of police and everything else. I didn't know what was going on."

"I'm sure there was a lot of activity. I was calling to find out if you knew if my mother is okay. I've been trying to find out but haven't been able to."

"Neveah…"

"Please, Miss Nancy. I need to know," Neveah teared up as she wondered if Miss Nancy had bad news to share. "My mother said she thought she might be killed if the police caught up with her and I just want to know if she's okay or… not."

"I really don't know, honey."

"Did you see them take her away?"

"I saw them take Otis away but I didn't see her at all. I don't think she was at the house when the police got over here. They tell me they found her walking over on the south side, but she refused to surrender. Since they thought she was dangerous, they had their guns out and when she fought back, they shot her. I don't know any more than that and I'm not sure if that's even true."

Neveah's sobs flowed. "Miss Nancy, I wish this whole thing hadn't happened. I feel like my whole life is messed up. This is just too much."

"I wish things were different, too, honey, and I'm sorry I don't have the answers you're looking for. No matter what happens, God is watching over you. Believe that."

Once again someone had mentioned God. Who is this God and where had he been when she needed Him is what Neveah wanted to know?

CHAPTER 14

Neveah laid in bed trying hard to get to sleep. For some reason, her mind wouldn't stop running all over the place. She cleared her mind to attempt to settle it down enough so she could sleep. She turned over in the bed as she felt herself relax.

Just as Neveah nodded off, she heard house shoes shuffling. Her eyes fluttered open a little and she noticed a figure in her room, moving toward her. When the movement stopped, she heard pants unzipping. Her breathing sped up as she anticipated what would happen next. She heard pants hitting the floor and even the sound of house shoes landing on the floor as each leg came out of the pants.

She blinked a couple of times in an attempt to assure herself of what she was seeing. She couldn't make out who it was, but she was sure they didn't belong there. She watched silently as the person advanced.

Resisting the urge to respond as she normally would, based on the pattern established each time Otis violated her, Neveah instead curled into the fetal position. The silhouette stopped moving. The standoff continued. Finally, the invader took another step forward, causing Neveah to sit up in bed.

"No, this can't be happening," she yelled, scaring her visitor causing them to leave the room. "Leave me alone! I'm not dealing with this anymore, Otis! I thought you were dead!"

Neveah whimpered as Bethany entered the room and turned the bedroom lamp on.

"What's wrong?" Bethany asked, positioning herself on the bed next to her foster daughter. Neveah leaned away from her as Bethany attempted to embrace the young woman.

"Just leave me alone. I want to be alone." Neveah rocked as she processed what had happened.

"I won't touch you but I'm not leaving."

"No, I want you to leave my room."

"Neveah, tell me what happened. Who's Otis?"

"I really don't want to talk about it."

"That's probably part of the problem. You need to get some of that out. Now, start by telling me what happened tonight."

Neveah finally opened up and told her foster mother what had occurred that night. She also felt comfortable enough to share what Otis had done to her numerous times, leading her to be placed in Bethany's home.

"I think you might be having night terrors. There was no one in your room when I came in here."

"It felt so real."

"That's how night terrors work. You might need some help dealing with the trauma from what you experienced. I'll place a call tomorrow to see if we can get something set up for you, if you're open to it."

"I don't know, Miss Bethany. I don't think I'll be comfortable sharing this stuff with a stranger. I'd be so embarrassed and ashamed."

"You have nothing to be ashamed of. You, my dear, are the victim. Besides, counselors have a way of getting you to open up. Just try it once and if it works for you, we'll keep going. How's that sound?"

"I'll try it out. Maybe it might help."

"Okay, I'm going back to bed and you should too. Don't worry. You're safe here." Bethany rose from the bed, turned off the lamp and stood at the door. "Good night, sweetheart. I'll see you in the morning."

"Good night, Miss Bethany." As Bethany closed the door, Neveah settled back in the bed. She closed her eyes and hoped she'd be able to relax and get some sleep.

CHAPTER 15

Bethany and Neveah walked through the shopping mall, looking for a few new outfits, but especially a dress for Neveah's birthday dinner. The invitees included her foster brothers, some of Bethany's family members and a few friends from Neveah's school.

"Thank you so much for this shopping spree. I really appreciate it," Neveah said, leading her shopping partner into a store.

"It's my pleasure. Do you like this?" Bethany asked, fingering the dress Neveah took off the rack.

"It is pretty. What do you think?"

"I think it's beautiful. With some nice shoes to match, it will be perfect. I think you should try it on."

"Okay," Neveah said, bouncing with excitement. She carried the dress to the changing room with Bethany following.

"I haven't heard you yelling in the middle of the night. I assume the nightmares must have slowed down at least."

"I still see someone in my room at night, but I can never make out if there's someone really there. I just try to tell myself it's my mind working overtime."

"Good. I hope it continues to improve. I really want you to feel safe in my home."

The two women obtained a fitting room and proceeded to get Neveah changed into the new dress. When they completed the change, Neveah stood in the mirror to examine the results.

The ruby red, above-the-knee length dress, with a flowing skirt made of chiffon layers, cinched waist, and sleeveless fitted bodice fit her taste and body perfectly.

Neveah twirled in order to watch the skirt flare out. "I love it! All I need is a pair of earrings and a bracelet and I'll be all set."

Bethany laughed. "It is beautiful. I think we have a winner. Let's get it and go so we have time to pick up shoes and accessories before the party." Bethany reached for the zipper in the back of the dress and unzipped it. Neveah changed back into her clothes and the two left the room to finish their purchase.

***

Applause greeted Neveah as she descended the stairs into the kitchen. The small group smiled as they hugged and complimented the now eighteen-year-old woman.

"Thanks, guys," Neveah said as she received the love of those gathered to celebrate her birthday.

"Come on in the dining room everyone," Bethany said. "Dinner will be served shortly. There are appetizers to hold you over until the meal is ready."

The crowd moved to the dining room as Bethany asked. Neveah followed Bethany to the kitchen.

"What do you need me to do?" Neveah asked Bethany.

Bethany turned toward Neveah with her hands on her hips. She cocked her head to the side and said, "You should be in there with your guests. I can handle this. You go enjoy yourself."

Neveah released a few quiet tears. Bethany noticed and moved closer to her foster daughter.

"Hey, what's wrong? Is everything okay?"

"I've never had a party like this before. My mother couldn't afford it. Thank you for taking me in and letting me live in this beautiful home, giving me all those gorgeous clothes, this awesome party and more than that, a lot of love. I'll never forget it as long as I live."

"Honey, it's my pleasure to do this for you. It's my assignment to love and care for young people like you and I'll always be there for you."

Neveah's tears flowed once again.

"What's wrong now?"

"I miss my mother. This is my eighteenth birthday and she's not here. I don't even know where she is and it bothers me."

"Oh, honey. I understand. It's okay to be concerned about your mother. I would probably feel the same way. If you need to go to your room and have a moment, I'm sure everyone will understand."

"I'll be okay. It would be rude to disappear like that. I'll just go to the bathroom and get myself together."

"Okay, I'll see you in a few." Bethany turned her attention back to food preparation. "Oh, and try to enjoy the party, all right?"

"I will Miss Bethany." Neveah left the kitchen and headed toward the lavatory down the short hall. The door was closed but she still heard a voice.

"Yeah, I don't even like her. I hope she gets moved to another home or something."

Neveah was sure the words spoken were about her and she recognized the voice as Collin's. She shook her head and decided to go to the upstairs bathroom since this one was occupied. Before she could walk away, Collin opened the door and stood face-to-face with her.

"Were you eavesdropping?"

"No, but I couldn't help but overhear you. What is your problem with me, anyway? I've never done anything to you."

"I can't stand a liar and I have proof you're a big one."

"I don't know what you're talking about. I think you're just jealous of my relationship with Miss Bethany and that's sad, because she loves us all the same."

"No, she doesn't. She loves you more because you're the only girl. But I told you I don't like a liar. I can't wait to tell Bethany what I know because I'm sure she'll send you away once she finds out who you really are."

"Whatever. Are you done in here?"

"No, I'm going back in."

"Fine, I'll just go upstairs."

***

During dinner, the conversation turned to Neveah's plans after graduation.

"I know this is your eighteenth birthday and all, but you'll also be graduating soon too."

"Yes, I'll be graduating early and then going to college sometime in the near future. Because of everything that happened, I'm a little behind on applying and all of that, but it's never too late to do it. Until then, I'll get a job and save some money."

"That's exciting. Do you have any idea what you want to major in?"

"I think we should talk about the 'everything that happened,' she mentioned," Collin said, using his fingers to form air quotes.

"I don't know where you're going with this, but I'm sure this is not the time or place for it." Miss Bethany shot a look at Collin.

"Why not now? I think everyone here at this little love fest ought to know who they're loving on."

"Collin! That's enough." Miss Bethany's voice rose to a volume Neveah had never heard her use.

"She lied about being there when her stepfather was killed. For all we know, she might be the killer."

The room fell silent until Neveah's voice broke the silence.

"Who told you that?" Neveah asked Collin.

"You did, sweetie. I overheard you talking to someone named Monique."

"Oh, so you were listening. Well, you heard wrong. I would never say I killed Otis because it's not the truth."

"Yeah, and I know you were having sex with him, too."

"Collin, go to your room please," Miss Bethany said through gritted teach, pointing toward the stairs.

"No, I want to hang around to watch you put her out. I wouldn't miss that for the world."

"Go, Collin," Miss Bethany repeated.

Bethany leaned over to Neveah who seemed to be frozen in place. "I'm sorry, honey. I don't know why Collin thinks I'm going to put you out but don't worry, it's not going to happen."

Neveah looked around the room at the guests who had just moments ago been celebrating her birthday. She wondered what they thought about her after Collin exposed her the way he did.

"Um, I don't know what to say. I guess Collin told the truth in a way, but he got some of the details wrong. I wasn't willingly having sex with my stepfather. He forced me. I'm not a killer, either. Today has been really emotional for me and I think I need a moment, so please excuse me. I'm going to head to my room. Thank you all for coming and helping me celebrate." Neveah quietly left the table.

When she walked through the hall upstairs, Collin stepped out of his room and smiled at Neveah. "Need help packing?"

Neveah didn't answer but kept moving toward her room. She entered and shut the door behind herself. She thought about Collin's suggestion that she leave and wondered if he was right. He was making her time there difficult for no reason whatsoever.

Suddenly, Neveah heard yelling. She recognized the voices as Collin's and Miss Bethany's. The argument lasted for at least five minutes during which guilt crept up on Neveah. She felt responsible for the disruption in the house and especially the one taking place down the hall. She had to imagine things were better before she arrived. This issue was adding to Neveah's emotional turmoil. Finally, Neveah heard a door slam and then silence.

There was a soft knock at her door to which Neveah responded with, "Who is it?"

"It's me."

"Come in."

Bethany walked in and moved quickly to Neveah's side. "I'm sorry. Collin had no right to tell everyone what happened. Don't worry. I smoothed everything over with the guests and everyone understood. And I told Collin that if he can't get it together, he has to go. I don't have to let him stay here so if he bothers you again, he's out."

"Miss Bethany, I don't want to be the cause of him having to leave. I just want him to stop harassing me and leave me alone."

"That's the kind of young lady you are. But it wouldn't be your fault if he had to go. It would be because of his behavior. You understand?"

"Yes." Neveah bowed her head as if in prayer.

Bethany softly touched Neveah's chin, turning her face toward her. "Aside from Collin, did you enjoy your party?"

"It was awesome, Miss Bethany. Thank you again."

"I'm glad to hear it. Now, there are unopened gifts downstairs. What do you say we go down there, have some cake and ice cream and open them?"

"They left gifts?"

"Yes, they did."

"I guess I should open them."

"Yes, I think you should."

The two laughed as they left Neveah's room, heading to open the gifts.

CHAPTER 16

Neveah sat in a chair in the family room, reading a book. She loved to read. It was one of the things her mother instilled in her from a young child. She flipped the page as Collin walked into the room. He plopped into a chair across from her and stared at her while popping grapes into his mouth one at a time, smacking his lips. Neveah wished he would go away but knew he wouldn't. Making her nervous was his goal. She'd never encountered someone who was so bent on causing her upset for no reason. She kept her eyes on her book while considering moving to her room to continue reading in peace. She decided against that because that's what Collin wanted and she wouldn't give it to him. This strategy wouldn't cause him to like her but it could quite possibly stop some of his attempts to intimidate her.

"You are so rude," Collin threw out, attempting to bait Neveah, who kept her eyes on her book and her mouth closed. "I know you hear me so let me tell you that I've decided to call the police about the lies you told them. They take that kind of thing seriously and will come here and take you away in a heartbeat. Even Bethany won't be able to stop that." Neveah continued ignoring Collin, who became visibly aggravated by her lack of response. He stood and sauntered over to Neveah. He slapped her book out of her hand, causing her to become angry as well.

"What do you want?" she yelled. "I do everything I can to stay out of your way, but you make it your business to hunt me down to bother me. You must want something. What is it?"

A huge smile spread across his face. "Nothing," Collin said. He laughed loudly as he left the family room.

Neveah shook her head after Collin left the room. *What was that all about?* Neveah wondered. She picked her book up from the floor and read until her eyes began to feel heavy. Neveah went to her room, careful not to make too much noise passing the room Collin shared with Sean. She didn't want to encounter Collin again that night.

Later, Neveah stirred, sensing the presence of someone in her room in the middle of the night. She turned over on her back and looked around the room. After her eyes adjusted to the darkness, she made out a figure standing by the door. Feeling this was obviously another nightmare, she relaxed, turned back over in the bed, and closed her eyes. After a few moments, Neveah felt a hand moving up her thigh. She struggled to determine whether this was really happening or if it was her imagination. When she felt a touch where her thighs met, her body betrayed her, causing her to shift her weight and lay on her back. Then her eyes flew open, her heart raced, and her mind went back to the many nights Otis invaded that space.

Suddenly, she felt the weight of someone lying on top of her, who began speaking. "You've been asking for this and now, I'm going to give it to you."

Neveah realized the experience she was having was real and began struggling with the intruder.

"Get off me!" she yelled, attempting to push the person off of her.

"Oh, come on. I know you like this kind of thing," the voice responded.

"No. I. Don't." Neveah continued to push and shove, trying to get out from under the intruder. She attempted to punch her assailant in the face.

The man grabbed her hands and pinned them over her head. He lowered his face to hers and she felt his tongue pressing against her lips.

"I'm going to make you scream my name," he said, pulling at his sleep shorts, then tugging upward on her gown.

"No, stop," she screamed, twisting her body to make it difficult for him to complete his apparent plan.

"I won't stop until I'm done. God, this is going to be so good."

"Miss Bethany," Neveah screamed. "Help!"

"Why would you go and do that? You're going to ruin this. Oh, wait. Bethany's a hard sleeper. She probably didn't even hear you."

The lights turned on, allowing Neveah to see Collin's face. Bethany stood at the door, disgust etched across her face.

"Get off of her," she uttered through gritted teeth.

Collin released Neveah's hands and rolled off of her. "We could've had a good time but you had to go and mess things up."

"Why in the world would you do this? You don't even seem to like Neveah," Miss Bethany asked.

"I don't like her but I like her body."

"Collin, I told you that if you didn't get it together, you were going to have to go. This is it. You need to leave in the morning."

"But you can't put me out. I don't have anywhere to go," Collin whined.

"I'm sorry you don't have anywhere to go, but I have to provide a safe living environment for everyone that lives here and you just showed me you're unwilling to be a part of that. This is not news to you. I told you what would happen if you attacked Neveah again. I don't know where you're going to go, but you must leave this house."

"Why can't she leave? She's the problem." Collin's face turned red as he jabbed his finger at Neveah.

"She must not be that big of a problem considering what I just saw you trying to do with her."

Neveah broke from her trance and went to her closet. She pulled out hangers with clothes on them and threw them across the bed, interrupting the verbal volleying between Bethany and Collin.

Bethany approached Neveah, touching her on her arm. "What are you doing?"

"I appreciate everything you've done to make me comfortable here, but this whole thing caused me to think I need to move out."

"Absolutely not. I'm not going to let you leave. You don't know what it's like out there in the streets."

"I don't feel safe here anymore. I just can't stay here after what happened tonight and all those other nights Collin was in my room."

"How will you live? You haven't even graduated from high school, yet. You don't have a job either."

"I have a little money my mama gave me so I can probably get a place and live for a bit while I look for a job. I'll try to stay close by so I can stay in the same school. But, Miss Bethany, I know it's time for me to go. Too many memories of what happened to me all of those years with Otis. I hope you'll understand and support my decision."

"Collin, I need you to go to your room and start packing your things. I expect you to leave in the morning."

Collin stomped out of the room. But not before speaking to Neveah. "I can't stand you. You are a whore and I'm glad your stepfather did what he did to you. You deserved every bit of it. I'm telling you, you'll get yours and that's a promise." He turned and left the room in a huff, slamming the door to the room he shared with Sean upon entry.

Tears fell from Bethany's chin as her eyes swept over Neveah's face. She grabbed the young woman gently by the chin and said, "You're not the type of young lady who belongs on the street. You won't be able to handle it. I know, because I was once homeless myself." She sat on Neveah's bed and pulled her down next to her. "Don't leave. You're a smart young lady and I think you know this move is not the right thing to do. I don't think you'll make it very long out there. Stay here. Finish high school. Go to college. Then you'll be prepared. I can't make you stay, but I do want you to know one thing. Even though you've been through a lot, God loves you. Don't ever forget it."

It was Neveah's turn to sob as she thought about this God Bethany spoke about. Where was He when everything was happening around her? Why hadn't He protected her from Otis or Collin? What value did God's love have if it allowed terrible things to happen to people?

Bethany continued, "Before you came here, God showed me your face and told me you would be coming. He told me what your needs would be and equipped me to provide them for you. Being out there, trying to make it on your own, is not the life God wants you to live. Collin will be gone tomorrow. Why don't you make your decision after that?"

Neveah considered Miss Bethany's proposal. She didn't want to leave. She was comfortable and well cared for. Besides, she wasn't sure where she would go considering Auntie Monique's place wasn't an option.

"Okay, I'll stay."

"Good. I was hoping you would say that. Let me go make sure Collin is preparing to leave."

CHAPTER 17

It had been a week since Bethany followed through on her promise and kicked Collin out of her home. It was not a pleasant experience, especially for Neveah. Collin elevated his harassment of her, blaming her for having to leave. Bethany had shed a few tears during the process, but stood her ground.

Neveah had spent that night trying to figure out how she would make it on her own. She realized the money her mother had given her from Otis' wallet wouldn't last long and a part-time job wouldn't be enough to support herself. If she quit school, she could work full-time and perhaps make enough money to pay for a small apartment, but she thought it might still be tight. However, if she got a place, she would be safe.

Neveah sat in a barstool at the counter in the kitchen, watching Bethany prepare dinner for the family. She marveled at the care the woman put into everything she did for those she loved. She carefully laid lasagna noodles over a layer of ricotta cheese in the deep dish. There would be no torn noodles. Neveah hoped one day, when she had a family of her own, she would be able to provide the level of care Bethany showed.

"Miss Bethany, who taught you to cook?"

"My mother and grandmother taught me everything I know. Why?" Bethany asked, spreading a layer of meat sauce on the dish.

"You're really good at it. I hope I'm a good cook when I get married and have children."

"Don't worry. I'll show you everything you need to know. You're pretty good already, but I think you'll be an even better cook than I am."

Bethany picked up the dish and moved it closer to the stove. Her cell phone rang just as she was opening the oven door.

"Can you answer that for me, please?" Bethany asked as she placed the lasagna in the oven.

"Hello," Neveah said, answering the phone.

"This is Metro General Hospital calling for Bethany Morris."

"Hold on a minute. Miss Bethany, it's the hospital calling."

"I wonder what this could be about. Put it on speaker," Bethany said as she closed the oven door and rushed to the phone. "Hello," she said. "This is Bethany."

"We have Collin Owens here in intensive care and we're contacting his next of kin. He's been in an accident. Can you come to the hospital right away?"

"Yes, I'll be there in twenty minutes." Bethany directed her attention to Neveah. "You heard I have to get to the hospital." Bethany moved around the kitchen, turning the oven off and putting a few things away. Miss Bethany constantly straightened the kitchen while she was cooking. "Are you coming with me?"

Neveah froze in place. "I don't know. Do you need me to go?"

"It's up to you, but I could use some support. It sounds serious."

"Okay, give me a minute. I'll get my shoes on."

***

"Mr. Owens was injured as the result of being hit by a car. He's going to need surgery and his recovery will be challenging," the doctor said, walking toward a set of doors. "He's right in here," she said, sliding her card through a reader, causing the doors to swing open.

"Excuse me," Neveah said. "Is there a waiting area somewhere close-by?"

"Yes, ma'am. It's right across the hall."

"Thank you. Miss Bethany, I'll wait for you in the waiting room."

"Okay, honey. I understand. I won't be long."

Neveah changed the channel on the television in the waiting room. It had been a couple of hours since Bethany disappeared behind the doors to check on Collin. She wondered what was going on back there. Perhaps she should have gone in as well. At least she would know how Collin was doing and how much longer they would be at the hospital.

She sat down to watch an episode of *Family Feud* as she waited. She wished she could be with her family. Her real family. She loved Miss Bethany, but she had some blood relatives she wanted to be with. But it was unclear whether Auntie Monique even wanted to see her. She would love to sit down and talk with her. Perhaps she would be able to clear things up with her. Hopefully, if Auntie Monique heard from Neveah's father, she would still let her know. It would be awesome to see and get to know him. Neveah hoped it would happen soon.

The doors Bethany had disappeared behind swung open and she came. Her face showed a little stress but at least she wasn't crying. Maybe Collin was better than first thought. Bethany appeared uneasy as she approached Neveah, who stood to find out what was happening.

"How is Collin?"

"They're going to keep him tonight for observation and run some more tests. If everything goes well, he'll be able to come home tomorrow," Bethany said, wringing her hands.

"That's good news." Neveah noticed Bethany's nervousness. "Why do I feel like there's something else?"

"Well, Collin has been staying in a shelter since he left my house, but he can't recover there. He's going to need to do that somewhere else."

Neveah nodded. "Your house?"

"I don't know what else to do. I wouldn't be able to face myself if I made him try to go through this process in a shelter. I mean, there's no one there to take care of him and he has to leave the shelter during the day. Where else would he go?"

Neveah shook her head in disbelief. She remained quiet as she thought about what she would say. Miss Bethany had promised Neveah she would be safe in her home. She stayed because Miss Bethany had begged her to. Now, because of Collin's accident, she was going back on that promise. How long would Collin be there? The bottom line was, even though Collin was injured, she didn't feel safe living in the same house with him.

Neveah grabbed her purse and left the waiting room without speaking a word to Miss Bethany. There was nothing to say. Miss Bethany followed silently.

CHAPTER 18

"Neveah, please talk to me," Miss Bethany said, jogging behind Neveah up the stairs. "I know you're upset but we've got to talk about this."

"You're wrong, Miss Bethany. There's nothing to talk about," Neveah said rushing down the hall to her room.

Both women entered Neveah's room and stood facing each other.

"Look, you know I would never knowingly put you in danger. I think I've proven that. But, how can I turn my back on Collin when he needs someone to help him?"

Neveah felt the desperation in Miss Bethany's plea. She knew Collin needed help, but she had a difficult time understanding how Miss Bethany could think she would be comfortable with being in the same house as Collin. He had already proven what he was capable of and yet Miss Bethany actually thought she could convince Neveah to take a chance on Collin not continuing his assaults on her. Miss Bethany cared about them both, so Neveah understood the woman's conflict. But Neveah's decision was clear.

"This is your house, so you don't owe me any special consideration."

"What does that mean, Neveah?"

"It means I can't expect you to look out for me anymore and it's okay. You feel the need to take care of Collin and I have to take care of myself."

"I don't like how that sounds. You're not thinking about leaving, are you? I still think you should stay. If I have to sleep on the floor in the hallway to keep Collin from coming in this room, I will."

"I don't know what I'm going to do."

"I'm sorry. I don't know what else to do. This is so unexpected and I know it feels like I'm not keeping my promise to you, but I'm trying. Please believe me." Bethany approached Neveah with outstretched arms. Neveah allowed Bethany to hug her. She even wrapped her arms around the woman as well.

"I love you, Neveah. I'm going to leave your room now to give you some space. I'll see you in the morning."

"I love you, too, Miss Bethany. I really do."

Bethany left the room and Neveah closed the door behind her. She laid back on her bed and thought about her situation. A plan developed and she decided to put it into action.

The next morning, Neveah rose early ahead of Bethany, and walked to an area where she thought there might be a room or small apartment she could afford to live in. It wasn't very far from Bethany's house, so she hoped she would still be able to go to the same high school.

She walked down a couple of streets looking for signs indicating a room was available for rent. When she turned the corner, she encountered a man walking his dog. The dog began barking at Neveah as soon as he saw her. When she got closer, the dog bared its teeth at her.

Neveah stopped walking. "Sir, can you get your dog?"

"She's just making a lot of noise. She doesn't bite."

"She has teeth, doesn't she?"

"You've got a point there. I'll make sure she doesn't get close to you," the man said as he wrapped the leash around his hand to shorten it. He moved the dog to the side away from Neveah. "Go ahead. I got her."

Neveah walked past the man and his barking dog, who was now lunging at her and jumping up and down. "Thank you," she said when she got past them.

"You're welcome. Hey, what are you doing out here walking around so early? I know you don't live around here because I've never seen you."

"I don't live too far away from here. I'm actually looking for an affordable place to rent. Do you know of a place?"

"You're in luck. I have an apartment in my building that's empty. If you want, you can follow me there and I'll show it to you. If you like it, we can talk about what you can afford to pay."

Neveah wondered if she should follow the man, but if she was going to move out, she needed to find someplace to move to. She felt the man was friendly enough so she decided to check out the apartment he had available.

As they approached the house, the man said, "By the way, I'm Quentin Brown and you are?"

"My name is Neveah."

"That's a beautiful name for a lovely lady." Quentin opened the door and stood to the side, allowing Neveah to enter first. He opened the door on the right and put the still barking dog inside.

She entered the somewhat run-down building and waited for the man to direct her to the apartment. The stairs had carpet on them that was dirty and matted in the center from wear and tear. The walls needed some repairs and a coat of paint. The lighting was dim, causing the small foyer to feel dreary and sad. In short, this was not Miss Bethany's house.

Neveah wondered if she was being hasty to leave such a beautiful home and loving environment to live someplace like this. Though Collin was a problem, perhaps Bethany would, indeed, make sure he left her alone this time. After all, Collin was now on notice that Bethany would put him out of the house. Since she was here, she would look at the apartment and find out what the rent would be then make her decision.

"Come on upstairs. That's where the vacancy is." He gestured for Neveah to head upstairs. He followed behind her and headed to the door on the left at the top of the stairs. He opened it and Neveah walked inside.

The space was very small but large enough for one person to live. Neveah looked through the tattered living room drapes that hung behind the brown plaid couch and saw the alley behind the building. Neveah walked around the end table with the lamp sitting on it into the kitchen through an opening in the wall. The stove and refrigerator were outdated but would serve the purpose. She exited the kitchen and went into a bedroom too small to hold anything larger than the full-size bed in the room.

"It will work for me. How much is the rent?"

"How much can you afford?"

"I really can't afford much. I'm still in school, so I don't have a job yet."

"Hold on. Are you eighteen? I can't rent to a minor, now."

"I'm eighteen. I just haven't graduated yet."

"From high school?"

"Yes."

"Why are you looking for a place?"

"I'm in foster care and need to leave the place I'm staying right now."

"I see. Is someone hurting you?"

"In a way."

"I think you need to stay where you are if there's any way possible. If not, I'll work with you on the rent until you can get yourself together and can pay full rent. But there is one condition."

"What is that?"

"You have to keep going to school and graduate. That's my condition for you living here."

"I can do that, Mr. Quentin. Thank you so much. I appreciate you giving me a chance. How should I contact you?"

Quentin dug into his pocket and pulled out a crumpled business card with his contact information on it.

"I'll be in touch soon. Thank you for your showing me the place. It's perfect for me."

CHAPTER 19

Neveah stood in the window and watched as Bethany and Sean helped Collin out of the car. She took a deep breath and exhaled in an attempt to tame the anxiety rising within her. She stepped away when Bethany spotted her. Neveah didn't want her to look in her eyes and see what she was thinking, feeling, and planning. No, she wanted to allow her to focus on getting Collin situated and then, Neveah would have Bethany's undivided attention.

She went to her room and closed the door. She heard them as they moved through the hall to get Collin to his bedroom, right down the hall from hers. Things got quiet then she heard a soft knock on her bedroom door.

"Who is it?" she asked, as if she didn't know it was Bethany.

"It's me," Bethany responded. "Can I come in?"

Neveah hesitated before responding. She wasn't sure she was ready for the conversation she knew was to come. She realized postponing it wouldn't do any good. It still needed to happen.

"Come on in," Neveah said from the chair in the corner of the room.

Bethany came in and quietly observed Neveah. The silence ensued for a few beats before Bethany brought it to a halt.

"Good morning," she said, breaking the ice.

"Good morning," Neveah responded.

"Can I talk to you for a few minutes?"

"Sure, have a seat."

Bethany took a seat on the bed. Her face showed serious concern.

How are you?" she asked. "I haven't seen much of you since we left the hospital."

"I'm okay. I see Collin made it in safely."

"He did, but I want to talk about you. I'm worried about you."

"Why? I'm just fine."

"Are you? I know you're upset about Collin being here."

"I can't say I'm excited about a molester living in the same house as me, especially considering what I experienced in the past."

"Look, you have every right to be upset. I'm sure you want to leave this house and never come back…"

"That's exactly what I plan to do. I found a place this morning not too far from here. I'm planning to move very soon."

"I was afraid you were going to do that. What can I do to change your mind? I care about you and feel this is a bad decision."

"I don't think you can change my mind at this point, Miss Bethany."

"Neveah, I don't think you know what you're getting into. In spite of what you might think, you are much safer here than you'll be out there. On top of all that, you're in unfamiliar territory and don't know anyone else in this area but me and my foster sons. Who will you go to if you need help? I can't watch out for you if you leave."

"I understand all of that, but I'm tired of being touched and fondled and all of that and with Collin back in the house… I just think I have to go."

"I don't agree, but it sounds like you've made up your mind. When are you leaving?"

"Since the apartment is empty, I should be able to get it when I pay my deposit."

"Hold on a second," Miss Bethany said, leaving the room.

A few moments later, she returned with a bottle of oil in her hand. She put a little of it on her finger and moved toward Neveah.

"Can I at least pray for you before you go?"

Neveah nodded, triggering Miss Bethany to rub the oil on Neveah's forehead. Then, laying her hand across it, she prayed for God's will to be done in her foster daughter's life, as well as her safety. Afterward, Miss Bethany hugged her and left the room without speaking another word.

Neveah realized this move was happening. The reality of it fell on her, causing Neveah to be nervous. A tear fell as she thought about how much she would miss her foster mother and living in her beautiful home. She knew the woman loved her. However, she'd made up her mind and she would follow through, with or without the fear.

CHAPTER 20

Neveah sat in the living room of her new apartment with her school books strewn out around her. She'd been able to maintain her attendance in the same high school she attended while she was at Miss Bethany's house. Her job search hadn't netted her a job that worked for her in terms of geography and available work hours. The money her mother had given her from Otis' wallet provided a meager existence that barely provided for her discounted rent and food. She was grateful utilities were included, since Mr. Quentin controlled those.

Miss Bethany had called Neveah several times over the past few weeks to check on her and see if she needed anything. Neveah had told her everything was fine though she could've used a few things like bed linens and more food. But when she moved out, she decided she was responsible for all of her needs regardless of what they were.

A knock at the door interrupted Neveah's thoughts. She went to the door and asked, "Who is it?"

"It's me. Mr. Quentin," the voice said on the other side of the door, prompting Neveah to open it.

"Hey, Mr. Quentin. What can I do for you?"

"You can pay your rent. That's what you can do."

"I already paid the rent. I've paid each week I've been here."

"I haven't gotten rent from you in a month. Now, I was willing to work with you on the amount of rent you paid, but you have got to pay what we agreed on."

"I've only been here three weeks so I couldn't possibly be a month behind. I haven't missed a week paying you. You don't remember?"

"How can I remember what didn't happen?" Mr. Quentin said, leaning his shoulder against the door opening.

"I paid you twenty-five each week I've been here, just like you asked."

"No, you haven't. You're going to have to pay up if you're going to stay here."

Neveah wondered what was wrong with Mr. Quentin. She made sure she paid her rent even if it meant she didn't eat. But he didn't remember and Neveah wondered why. The man never seemed to have any memory problems before. When he took her rent each week, he never said she was behind. He simply said, "Thank you."

"How much do you say I owe you?"

"A hundred dollars."

"I don't have that kind of money, Mr. Quentin! What is going on?"

"I already told you. Now, you need to get my money or you're going to have to leave," Mr. Quentin demanded as he left the apartment.

Neveah fell onto the couch and dropped her head into her hands. She didn't know what to do. She had the money but she needed to make it last until she could find a job that would pay enough for her to live a little more comfortably.

A thought came to mind and Neveah went to her phone. She called someone she hoped would help her.

"Hey, Neveah. How are you?"

"Not good, Auntie Monique."

"What's going on?"

"I had to move out the foster home."

"Oh, no!"

"I got a place, but my landlord is demanding I pay rent I already paid and I just don't have it like that. I'm trying to make the money Mama gave me stretch until I can graduate and get a job to take care of myself."

"You're going to have to pay the man and hold onto your receipts. All I can do is give you some money to get you through. Give me your Cash App, PayPal information or something so I can get it to you."

"I didn't call to ask for money. I just needed somebody to help me work through this issue with Mr. Quentin."

"Pay him, but remember to get a receipt each time you pay and hold onto them. That way you have proof you paid."

"All right. Thank you, Auntie Monique."

"Call me back if you change your mind about me sending you money."

Neveah disconnected the call, went to her purse and pulled out the bills she had left. She peeled off a hundred dollars and prepared to take it to Mr. Quentin. She stuck the rest of the money back in her purse. She went to her notebook and wrote a receipt, documenting the payment she was about to make.

She went to Mr. Quentin's apartment and asked him to sign the receipt before she gave him the money. He obliged her, then took the hundred dollars and closed the door.

CHAPTER 21

Neveah's graduation was taking place in just two weeks and she was excited. She had secured a part-time job with the promise it would become full-time after she graduated. Since she was graduating early, she would participate in the official ceremony in May. Once she got a little more established, she would explore the possibility of college as well. Something she and her mother had discussed her doing.

Bethany had called her and told her Collin was leaving again and she wanted Neveah to come back. Neveah thought about returning since Collin wouldn't be there, but she was enjoying her newfound independence which made her hesitant to do so.

Neveah settled into her bed with her back against the headboard to study for final exams. While she took the materials she needed from her backpack, she thought about her life over the past five months. Though she was healing from everything that happened, she was still in process.

Just as she opened her math book, she heard a knock at the door.

"Open this door, young lady. I come to get my rent."

It was Mr. Quentin asking for rent again. Neveah knew she didn't owe him but she couldn't figure out why he kept thinking she did. This time she was armed with receipts proving her payments since the last time he claimed she didn't pay the rent. She opened the door and let the man in.

"I don't know how you expect to live somewhere for free. I done told you time and time again you can't live anywhere for free. Now, where's my money?"

"Mr. Quentin, you keep doing this and I'm wondering what's going on. You accept my rent, sign the receipt and thank me for paying. Then you show up here saying I haven't paid you when you know I have."

"I don't know no such thing."

"I have proof that I paid. Let me get it." Neveah left the living room and went to her bedroom to get the receipts. She turned to leave but found Mr. Quentin standing in the doorway with a grin on his face. Not knowing what was happening, Neveah attempted to show him the payments she'd made.

"I don't know where you got those receipts from because I don't give receipts."

"I kept receipts, Mr. Quentin, and you signed each and every one of them acknowledging I paid you."

"Whose signature is that? It's not mine."

Neveah was truly concerned. *How could he deny he signed the receipts?*

Mr. Quentin began to move further into Neveah's bedroom, backing her up to the bed. His eyes seemed to drink in every inch of her body. Neveah could've sworn she even saw him lick his lips.

"I know you're probably having a hard time paying, but I'm a reasonable man. I won't evict you if you pay me."

"Mr. Quentin, I'm not giving you any more money until my next payment is due and that's next Friday."

"Oh, you're going to pay me one way," his eyes roamed across her breasts, "or another. If you know what I mean."

Neveah knew exactly what Mr. Quentin wanted, but she couldn't believe the man she met while he was walking his dog would approach her this way. She saw him as a father figure of sorts and now she found out he was just like most other men she knew. She realized he'd been faking memory loss so he could demand sex from her for payment of rent she didn't owe and didn't have the money for.

"I can't believe you, Mr. Quentin. Are you suggesting I sleep with you in order to pay rent you and I both know I don't owe you?"

"You know what I want and it ain't no sleep."

"I'm not paying you with money or sex."

"I know you don't have any place to go since you left that foster home and you wouldn't have been in foster care if you had family around somewhere who would take you in. So, why don't you stop pretending you have options and just give me what I want. I'll tell you what. You won't have to pay rent for every week you let me hit that."

"You have no idea what I've been through, Mr. Quentin. I'm tired and I'm not going to play this game with you."

"Welp, I guess you no longer have a place to stay."

"Why would you do that when I can pay you?"

"Not the way I want to be paid. I'll expect you to be out no later than Friday. It's a shame you feel the way you do. You could've had a free place to stay." He wiped the drool from his mouth and stomped out of the apartment, slamming the door behind him.

Neveah fell back on the bed and sobbed. She was so close to graduating and ran into another roadblock. She wondered why she seemed to attract men who wanted to take advantage of her sexually. This was a pattern and she didn't know how to break it. It felt as though she must be wearing a sign inviting that type of behavior. She didn't have time to explore that topic any further. Her most pressing issue was figuring out what she was going to do after Friday. Where would she live? How would she be able to get another place with dwindling funds? These were the things Neveah turned her focus to and away from men like Otis and Mr. Quentin.

Later, there was a knock at Neveah's door. Neveah hoped it wasn't Mr. Quentin again asking for rent payment. She was tired of dealing with him about this and had already decided to move out. She dragged herself to the door.

"Who is it?"

"I'm Leland, your landlord's son. I need to speak with you for a moment."

"I'm sorry, sir, but I don't know you so you'll have to talk to me through the door."

"I'm not here to hurt you. I need to explain something to you about my father's behavior. Please open the door."

Neveah thought for a few moments and decided to open the door. The man seemed sincere and credible, considering he mentioned Mr. Quentin's behavior.

Neveah opened the door and stared at a younger version of Mr. Quentin's face. This man was definitely related.

"Can I come in?" he asked. "I really don't want to discuss this in the hall."

"Sure, come in."

Leland entered Neveah's apartment and stood near the door.

"My father mentioned to me you hadn't been paying rent..."

"Let me stop you right there. I don't know what you and Mr. Quentin are trying to pull here, but I've paid more rent than I owe and it still wasn't enough. I'm moving out."

"Let me finish. I know you paid rent just like you said. My father has been diagnosed with the beginning stages of dementia, so he really believes you haven't paid. I'm here to refund you the amount you're out plus some for your trouble." He pulled three hundred dollars from his pocket and pressed it into Neveah's palm.

Tears sprung to Neveah's eyes. She was thankful that she had her money back and more. She would need it to get a new place.

"Thank you so much. I'll need this to get a new place."

"I was hoping you'd stay. My dad could really use the rent from this place. Why are you still leaving?"

"Not only did your father keep asking me for rent I already paid, but he also suggested I pay him with sex since I didn't have any more money. He actually followed me into my bedroom and backed me into my bed."

Leland slapped his forehead. "I can't believe he did that. My father wouldn't ordinarily do that. Trust me. He's not like that."

"I can't stay here after that. I wouldn't feel safe."

"I guess I don't blame you in that case. I'm sorry about what happened and I wish you luck in finding your next place. I'll let my father know you're moving out."

"Thank you for everything. Take care of your father."

"You're welcome and I will."

Leland stepped into the hallway to leave but before Neveah closed the door, Mr. Quentin appeared next to his son.

"Did she give you the rent, Leland? She's always behind. I can't afford to let her live here free."

"I took care of things, Dad. Don't worry. Let's go downstairs. I need to talk to you."

Leland winked at Neveah and she returned the gesture. She felt bad for Mr. Quentin and his son. Once dementia progressed, life became difficult to manage. She'd watched her mother go through it with her grandmother. Neveah closed and locked the door behind her. She decided to start packing so when the time came, she'd be ready to leave.

CHAPTER 22

Neveah dragged her bags from the apartment she'd only stayed in for four-and-a-half weeks. As she descended the stairs, she saw Mr. Quentin standing in the doorway of his apartment. She turned her glance from him quickly to avoid the eye contact he obviously wanted.

"You sure you want to leave? My offer still stands."

"I'm not interested. I just needed a place to stay, not what you're suggesting."

"Where are you going? Back to your foster home?"

"I don't know. I'll figure something out."

"I don't understand why you would rather live on the street than giving me a little taste. It's not as bad as you might think. Heck, you might even enjoy it."

"Bye, Mr. Quentin," Neveah said as she pulled her bags from the building.

She stood outside the building and looked in one direction first and then the other. She remembered there was a shelter downtown, so she decided to walk there. As she moved in that direction, she wondered what would happen to her. She'd never lived in a shelter but she'd heard they were filthy, dangerous, and generally not a place anyone would want to be. Neveah thought even if those things were true, it had to be better than living with someone who demanded sex for rent, or living on the street.

After walking for about thirty minutes, Neveah arrived at the shelter. It was a beige brick building with a black wrought iron fence around it. She pushed the button attached to the gate, assuming it would get the attention of someone inside who could help her.

"I'm sorry. We don't intake anyone until five o'clock. Come back then and we'll see if we can find a place for you."

Neveah's breath caught in her throat as she realized she had several hours before they could possibly help her. "Sir, I need a place to stay right now. I have no place to go."

"Ma'am, I understand, but I don't make the rules. Maybe you should check the church across the street. They have a church service on Fridays at noon. They might be able to help you sooner than I can."

Neveah turned and looked at the church. "Thank you, sir. I'll go over there now since I have no place else to be."

"Good luck to you. If you can't find anything else, come back and we'll see what we can do. If I were you, I'd get here early to increase your chances of getting in."

"You mean even if I get here extra early, I still might not get in?"

"I'm sorry to say it happens. It all depends on the demand."

Neveah waited for the light to change so she could cross the street. She then walked up to the front door of the church and pulled on the door. It didn't give. Apparently, no one was there yet. Neveah looked at her watch and discovered it was just ten o'clock. She didn't know what she would do for two hours. Her stomach growling let her know she should use some of her time to eat. There was a small diner a couple of blocks away so she decided to go there and get something cheap since she was still nursing the remaining money she had.

The young woman entered the diner dragging her bags with her. The restaurant hosted a bar-height counter around the space where guests dined. She found a stool in the corner that would allow her a place to stash her bags while she ate.

"Ma'am, there's no loitering allowed in here. You're going to have to leave," the waitress said, approaching Neveah, moving her hands in a sweeping motion toward the door. "Come on, you've got to go."

Neveah slowly stood from the stool. "I just want to get some food. Why do I have to leave?"

"We have a problem with homeless people coming in here hanging around, causing our paying customers to be uncomfortable. There are places for people like you and this isn't one of them."

"I might be homeless, but I have money to pay for a meal. That's the reason I came here, to get something to eat."

"When I saw you with those bags, I thought you were just coming in here to hang out. If you're going to buy something, make yourself comfortable and I'll be with you in a few minutes to take your order." The waitress walked away, giving Neveah time to look at the menu and decide what she wanted.

"Have you made a decision?" the waitress asked a few minutes later with her notepad and pen ready.

"I'll have the special. I want scrambled eggs, wheat toast and turkey bacon, please. I'll have water to drink."

"Thank you. We'll have that right out to you."

***

After changing clothes in the bathroom at the diner, Neveah walked up to the church. Several people were moving about. Some held conversations while others were heading inside. A couple of them examined her and seemed to find her lacking. Neveah made eye contact with several of them, smiled and greeted them but not one of them acknowledged her presence.

She stepped into the building hoping to find the help she was told she could receive there. A man stood at the entrance to the sanctuary with a red cup in his hand. She thought he was an usher who would greet her and take her to her seat.

"Good morning," she said, greeting the man who responded by looking at her and barely nodding his head. Neveah didn't feel any warmth coming from him whatsoever.

A woman appeared seemingly out of nowhere and headed toward Neveah. Her demeanor was both welcoming and helpful. "Good morning! Is that a donation for the homeless?" she asked, pointing at Neveah's bags.

"No, ma'am. I am the homeless."

The woman took Neveah in and responded, "You don't look homeless."

"I may not look like it, but I am. Can you help me?"

"Come with me," she said, heading toward a hallway that led to some offices. "How did you hear about us?"

"The man I talked to at the shelter across the street told me I might be able to get some assistance since he can't help me until later."

The lady released a breath and shook her head. "I wish he would stop doing that. We don't really provide that kind of help," she told Neveah, who was taking in the "Jesus loves you" posters as they walked down the hallway.

The two entered an office and the woman closed the door, then took a seat behind the desk. The woman clasped her hands in front of her on the desk. "Tell me what's going on."

"I just came out of the foster care system and got my own apartment. I had to move out this morning because I was having problems with my landlord."

"Okay, so you need a place to live."

"Yes, ma'am. It would even be helpful if I could get a hotel room for a few nights. I don't know if I'll be able to get a bed at the shelter and I have nowhere else to go. I don't even have to eat if I can just have a safe place to sleep."

"Do you have a job?"

"Yes, part-time."

"Why don't you get a full-time job?"

"I can only work part-time while I'm still in high school. I graduate soon and then I'll move to full-time."

"I see. Are you a member of this church? I don't think I've seen you here before."

"No, I'm not a member of any church."

"Do you believe in God?"

"I don't know much about Him."

"I'm sorry, we can't help you."

"Why?"

"You have a job, which means you should be able to take care of yourself."

"But, like I said, it's only part time until I graduate."

"We don't care why you can't work full-time. The other problem is we generally only help those who are members of our church. We do make exceptions sometimes, but only for those who share our beliefs and clearly you don't."

"But…"

"I'm sorry, young lady. I suggest you go back to the shelter at the appropriate time and hopefully you can get a spot over there. You're welcome to stay for service, if you'd like. God bless you!" The woman came from behind her desk and opened the door, clearly dismissing her.

Neveah left the office and decided to stay for the service since she had time. She entered the sanctuary and found a seat in the back. She heard the minister speak about the need to minister to those who needed help, although no one seemed to care that she was a soul who desperately needed some. All she wanted was to find some stability and comfort. She'd never gone to church that she could recall, but she'd heard about it. How could she ever become a part of this club if no one would even acknowledge her presence? How could she connect with the people to the point someone might whisper the password she needed to gain entry into this "secret society" called church? Obviously, she wouldn't find help here. They were too busy "doing ministry" as the speaker preached about, to notice a person in need of ministry had just walked in the door in a black skirt, pink button-down shirt and black patent leather shoes.

After a while, she checked the time to ensure she wouldn't be late getting in line at the shelter. She needed to make sure she was in the best position possible to get a bed for the night. She got up, took her bags and moved to the exit. Right past a picture of a man she assumed was God, with His hands outstretched towards her as though He was willing to help. What a joke, considering there was obviously no help forthcoming.

CHAPTER 23

Neveah settled into the shelter for the night. Her surroundings included about fifty beds and about half as many pallets on the floor. The men, women, and children were pressed into the small space so tightly, there was barely room to move around. Neveah was one of the lucky ones, if one could call it that, because she got a bed. She stuffed her bags underneath the bed and wondered what would happen next.

A man came into the noisy area and yelled, "Dinner time."

Everyone stopped what they were doing and moved. Neveah followed them eagerly to fill her empty stomach. She observed the long rows of rectangular tables covered with plastic table coverings and metal chairs slid up to them. The line was long but moved quickly. The people behind the counter passed a plate between them, placing dollops of food on it. When it got to the end, they passed it to the next person in line and started the process all over again until everyone was served.

Neveah poked at the meat loaf and mashed potatoes. They weren't her favorites, so she started eating the green beans from her plate.

"Are you going to eat that?" a male voice asked.

Neveah looked around to see where the voice came from. She saw a young man sitting behind her, pointing at her plate.

"Don't like meatloaf?"

"Not really."

"I'm Wesley by the way. You are?"

"Nice to meet you. I'm Neveah."

"I can tell you're new here, so let me give you some advice. You need to figure out how to eat whatever they put on your plate because there's no more food until the morning. That's got to hold you over until you get back here tomorrow evening, assuming you get back in. But, if you just can't stomach it, I'll take your share. Just let me know." He turned back around and focused on his plate. Neveah thought about what the cute guy said and took a few bites. After all those years she refused to eat her mother's meatloaf, she discovered she enjoyed it once she began eating it.

She stood to put her tray away and was approached by one of the ladies who was serving food.

"Hi, dear. I'm Jorga, Just like the state. Would you mind pitching in to wash dishes tonight?"

"I don't mind and my name's Neveah. I'd like to go to the bathroom and wash my hands first. Where is the nearest restroom?"

"Come on. I'll show you."

The two walked a few steps before the woman stopped and turned to Neveah.

"You look awfully young to be here alone. Why are you here?"

Neveah wondered if she should confide in the woman with the understanding eyes and graying around her hairline.

"I had to leave my foster family and my landlord evicted me." A tear silently trekked down her cheeks. She hadn't allowed herself to think about all of the things she'd endured in such a short period of time, focusing instead on overcoming her hardship. "I'm just trying to hang in there until I can finish high school so I can work full-time and hopefully get a place to live."

The woman exhaled a short breath. "Whew, that's a lot. Don't you have any family that could help you out?"

"I don't know where my mother is, but I have an aunt in Louisville and a father I've never met. Nobody seems to know where he is."

"Why don't you get in contact with your aunt? I can't see anyone denying help to a family member."

"She doesn't want to take me in. For some reason, she thinks I'll go after her boyfriend. I've never even met the man. Besides, I was raised to believe this woman was my mother's friend. I only recently found out she was actually my father's sister. I didn't even know my father was alive until then. I don't think I trust her. After all that's happened, I'm at the point I don't trust anyone, really." Neveah chuckled through her tears. "I'm not sure why I'm telling you all of this though."

Jorga squeezed Neveah's hand. "My guess is no one even cared enough to ask about how you're feeling. So, when I did, you just released what was on your mind and your heart. Honey, most of these people that run this shelter just see you as a homeless person. Someone who didn't make the best decisions in life so they think you deserve what you get. I don't see people that way. There's always a story under the story."

"Maybe you're right. I feel so alone and I'm scared."

"I can see why. Let's go get these dishes done. Maybe we can come up with a solution that will get you out of this shelter. You don't belong here."

CHAPTER 24

"Miss Jorga, you're looking at a high school graduate," Neveah excitedly announced to her newfound friend and mentor.

"Congratulations! That's awesome, baby. We need to celebrate. What do you want to do?" Jorga said, wiping down one of the long dining room tables.

"I don't need a celebration. I'm just happy to move on with my life and hopefully, out of this shelter."

"You should always mark your special moments. Let me know the next day you'll be off and we'll plan to do something, okay?"

"If you put it that way, we'll celebrate." Neveah began to rub her lower abdomen.

"Are you okay?"

"Just some cramping."

"Is it your period?"

Neveah thought for a few moments. "I don't know."

"When was the last time you had a period?"

"I don't know the answer to that question either. I've been so busy trying to survive, I haven't even thought about it."

"Hmm. Are you sexually active?"

"No, Miss Jorga. That is the last thing on my mind," Neveah responded, sweeping around a table.

"That's good because you don't need to be doing that right now. You have other things to deal with."

"It does hurt pretty badly, but I don't have time to be sick." Neveah moaned as she experienced a stronger cramp.

Miss Jorga rushed to Neveah's side. "Okay, if your cycle doesn't start soon, you need to get checked out."

"I don't have insurance. How will I afford to see a doctor?"

"You can't get insurance at your job? You're going to be full-time soon, right?"

"Yeah, but it's expensive. I think I'd be better off taking a chance on not needing the insurance than losing all that money from my paycheck just in case I get sick. I'm still going to need every penny I get to live on. It's not like I'm making a whole lot of money."

"I do understand. God will make a way."

Neveah decided not to respond to Miss Jorga's comment about God helping her let alone making it so she could see a doctor. Her experience was that He wasn't the least bit interested in her or her problems, if He even existed.

CHAPTER 25

Two weeks later, Neveah found herself sitting in Miss Jorga's doctor's office. She was nervous because this visit could change her life in a number of ways. She could have some sort of serious disease that would require surgery or some sort of treatment she couldn't afford. At any rate, her period had not made an appearance and she was still having symptoms.

"Don't be nervous, honey," Miss Jorga advised, squeezing Neveah's hand. "Everything is going to be okay."

Neveah shot the woman a brief smile. "If you say so."

"I say so," Miss Jorga pressed her hand onto Neveah's bouncing knees. "Now, relax."

Neveah relaxed as much as she could waiting for the doctor to call her back.

"Neveah, come on back."

Neveah rose, but Miss Jorga didn't.

"Aren't you coming?"

"You want me to?" Miss Jorga asked, scooting to the edge of her seat.

"I don't think I can do this alone."

Miss Jorga followed the nurse and Neveah into an examination room. The nurse questioned Neveah about her reason for the visit before leaving her to wait for the doctor.

Five minutes later, the doctor appeared and interviewed Neveah. After, getting what there was of her medical history documented, he took her temperature, pulse, heart rate, and measured her oxygen levels. Afterward, he questioned her about her symptoms. He decided to draw some blood, take a urine sample, and examine her. With her blood drawn and the urine sample given, Neveah waited in a gown on the exam table for the doctor to return for the physical examination.

The doctor returned and asked Neveah to lay back on the bed. He pressed her belly and asked, "Does it hurt when I press here?"

"No, it doesn't."

"Doctor, we have some test results. Would you like them now?"

"Yes, please."

The nurse opened the door wide enough to pass a file folder to the doctor who immediately opened it and read its contents. He closed it and smiled at Neveah and Miss Jorga.

"Congratulations, you're pregnant."

Neveah's eyes got big and her hand flew to her mouth. Miss Jorga came to her mentee's side and wrapped her arms around her. Neveah wondered why the doctor congratulated her as if this was good news. This was not a celebratory moment. Neveah had no idea how she would be able to have a baby, given her current circumstances. If this God people talked about was real, this would be a good time for Him to reveal Himself. Otherwise, Neveah was in big trouble.

***

"What am I going to do, Miss Jorga? I can't take care of a baby!" Neveah said, walking to Miss Jorga's car.

"You'll do what you have to do. First, you're going to get insurance as soon as you can since you'll need prenatal care. We'll get through this one step at a time." Miss Jorga waited a beat before continuing. "By the way, I thought you said you weren't sexually active."

"I'm not. My mother's husband forced me to have sex with him all the time. I've never been with anyone else."

"That's a terrible thing to go through. I had no idea that had happened to you."

"It's not something I talk about."

"You'll have to contact him and let him know he needs to help you with this child."

"I can't. He's dead."

Miss Jorga dropped her head and shook it. "I'm so sorry. That's a lot for anybody to handle. But don't worry. You're not alone. You have me now. You and the baby are going to be just fine."

After Miss Jorga dropped Neveah off at work, Neveah spent the afternoon thinking about her predicament. Knowing it was time to clock out was a relief. She could get back to the shelter and relax until dinner time.

As she stood waiting to officially clock out, her boss walked up. "Clocking out?" he asked, before running his finger down the schedule. "I thought you were working until seven o'clock tonight."

"No, sir. I never work that late."

"It's right here. You're full-time now, right?"

"No one told me about the change in my schedule. I can't work that late because of my situation."

"I'm sorry, you'll have to work it tonight, because we don't have the coverage otherwise."

"You don't understand. If I don't leave now, I won't have a place to sleep tonight."

"Won't have a place to sleep? Neveah, what's going on?"

Neveah explained her predicament to her manager. He shook his head and appeared concerned as she shared her story.

"I'm so sorry. I didn't know all of that was going on. The other manager shouldn't have scheduled you like this without discussing it with you first, but we really need you tonight. Is there any way you can work around that?"

"I don't think so. The shelter is pretty strict about that. Let me make a call to see if they can make an exception."

"Okay, please let me know."

Neveah retrieved her cell phone from her locker and placed her call. "Miss Jorga, I need a favor. I hope you can help me. My schedule got changed without me knowing it and I won't be able to get off until seven."

"That's after intake time. What are you going to do?"

"Can you talk to someone and see if they'll make an exception this one time?"

"Let me see if Damon can hold a spot for you and I'll call you right back."

"Okay. Thank you."

A few moments later, Neveah's phone rang. It was Miss Jorga. "Okay, he's saving a bed for you. Make sure you call me when you get here so I can tell him to let you in."

"That's a relief. Thank you so much, Miss Jorga. I really appreciate your help."

"There's never a problem when it comes to you. I love you. I'll see you in a little while."

Neveah called Miss Jorga as the bus arrived at the stop before hers. The phone rang until it went to voicemail. She disconnected the call and tried again. Still no answer. She got off of the bus right across the street from the shelter and walked to the entrance. She was glad the bus stop was so close since rain was falling heavily as a thunderstorm moved through the area. She pushed the bell and waited for someone to answer. She rang again and finally got an answer.

"Intake is not until tomorrow at five o'clock."

"Um, this is Neveah and Miss Jorga made arrangements for to save a bed for me. She told me to call when I got here and she would tell Damon to let me in. I called but she didn't answer."

"I'm sorry to tell you, but Miss Jorga suddenly fell ill about an hour ago and I don't know anything about this arrangement you're talking about."

"Oh, no! Is she okay?"

"They think it was a massive heart attack. The last I heard was she was in a coma and things weren't looking good. That's all I know right now."

"Is Damon there? He was supposed to save me a place."

"He had an emergency at home and had to leave."

"Well, I have nowhere else to go and Miss Jorga has my belongings in there somewhere. There's no place for me to sleep? Not even on the floor?"

"I'm sorry, Neveah but we're overflowing because of this weather tonight. You know if I could take you in, I would. Get here tomorrow on time and I'm sure we'll be able to find you a space. I'll see if I can find out where Jorga put your things, so you can at least have those. Be safe out there."

Neveah fell against the door and bawled. The weight of everything she'd been through and was going through caused a breakdown she wasn't sure she would be able to climb out of. The tears rivaled the drops of rain rolling down her face. Eventually, she pulled herself away from the door and sat on a step to figure out what she should do next. She was motherless, fatherless, homeless, and pregnant. Even Miss Jorga had exited her life, leaving Neveah all alone. She felt like giving up.

As the rain soaked her hair and clothes, she wondered what she'd done to unleash this kind of trouble on her life. She rubbed her slightly swollen belly and realized she needed to create a better life for herself and her baby away from this shelter. She would love this child, though he or she hadn't been conceived from a loving relationship but from sexual abuse.

Neveah looked around, thinking she'd heard something behind her. When she returned her gaze in front of her, she saw a woman standing there. Neveah jumped, startled by the young woman's sudden appearance.

"Hi," the young woman said, pulling her rain-soaked baseball cap down further on her head. "Are you okay?"

"I'm fine," Neveah responded, attempting to sound more confident than she felt.

"Why are you sitting out here, then?"

"Why are you out here in this weather?"

"I walk by here every now and then to see if there's someone who didn't make it into the shelter. Is that why you're out here?"

"Actually, it is."

"Where's your family?"

"I don't have any family around here. Why?"

"I was just like you, out here in the street homeless, jumping from shelter to shelter trying to piece my life together, so I know what you're going through. Someone told me about The Family of Saints, so I went to check it out. Joining them was the best decision I've made in a long time. We'll be your family. That's what you need, the stability and support of people who care about you. Why don't you come and see for yourself? I'm sure you won't regret it."

"Is it a church or something? I don't do the whole church and God thing."

"It's nothing like that. We're a family. Come check it out. The way I see it, you have nothing to lose."

CHAPTER 26

The next morning, Neveah had her belongings and an update on Miss Jorga, who was in critical condition but still alive. At least there was comfort in that. She contacted her job and told them she was quitting. She hated to leave on such short notice, but she had to get her life together for herself and her baby and The Family of Saints appeared to be her best opportunity.

She boarded the rickety, yellow former school bus, along with several other people and headed for The Family of Saints compound. Neveah was a little scared but no more than she had been since she became homeless. She hoped her relationship with The Family of Saints would solve all of her problems. She had been assured she wouldn't have to worry about a place to lay her head, food to eat, or her personal safety and that was a huge weight off of her shoulders.

The bus left the city limits and gave way to vast fields and sparse housing. After a couple of hours, the bus pulled onto a bumpy unpaved road that ran through a thick forest. Neveah wondered how much further they needed to go, since the bus driver didn't seem to care about how jarring it was when he hit the deep holes in the road at full speed. Neveah rubbed her belly and hoped her unborn child wouldn't be too disturbed by all of the jostling.

Finally, the bus entered a clearing, revealing a collection of small white buildings. The bus slowly approached a clearing in the middle of the buildings and came to a stop. People appeared, surrounding the bus and clapping. Neveah looked out of the window at them, saw their smiling faces, and immediately felt welcome. She felt herself relax as she grabbed her belongings and prepared to get off the bus.

As each person exited the bus, they were greeted by a representative of The Family of Saints and shown to one of the buildings. Inside, there was a number of doors. Behind each door was an apartment complete with full bathroom, bedroom, kitchen, and living room. Each room was furnished but sparsely decorated.

"Ma'am, I am Ellis, your escort. Your presence is expected at a welcome ceremony this afternoon. I will bring you some attire for the occasion in about thirty minutes. You will find the kitchen stocked with a selection of items we hope will be to your liking. If there is something you want or need, please let us know and welcome to The Family of Saints."

"Thank you," Neveah responded.

Ellis left her space, giving Neveah time to observe her new surroundings. It was immaculate and comfortable, a hundred percent better than the shelter. Things were looking up so far. Since Neveah didn't sleep well the night before, she decided to try out the bed in her new apartment and take a nap. She wanted to be alert for the ceremony.

***

The crowd buzzed as they gathered for the ceremony. Neveah figured there were roughly one hundred people there. Her escort appeared and moved her to a chair in front of the crowd. Before her were two chairs made out of what appeared to be tree trunks sitting upon stilts raising them at least ten feet up. Neveah assumed the leaders of the group would sit there, though it would be interesting to see how they got up into those seats.

There was a group of older women standing in front of the chairs, who quieted the crowd when they began singing loudly. The majority of those in attendance obviously knew the song because they sang and danced along with them.

Another group of women and men lined up two-by-two came through the crowd followed by a colorfully dressed couple, causing the crowd to erupt with cheers and clapping. The woman wore a print caftan and a matching headpiece with feathers, jewels, and ribbon. The man wore a dashiki-style shirt with a sash around his waist, matching knee-length pants, and a crown with jewels. Neither wore shoes, but both had decorative anklets to complete their look.

Men stood in front of each chair and formed a human ladder, allowing first the woman then the man to climb up and sit in their chair. Afterward, the men climbed down and marched away, presumably to wait until they needed to help the couple down.

Neveah noticed the couple eyeing the group of newbies as if to evaluate them. The man's eyes landed on a man sitting a couple of seats away from her, intently staring at him. She watched as his eye color changed from gray to brown, causing Neveah to question whether she really saw what she believed she'd just seen. He summoned one of the guys over and pointed to the man. The guy walked over and led the man away, letting

Neveah know she had indeed witnessed the man's eyes change colors.

The singing, cheering and clapping stopped, giving way for the woman to speak.

"I am Supreme Saint Nasia Poole. Chief of this wonderful assembly, The Family of Saints."

"I am Supreme Saint Akadeus Poole and I am the Assistant Chief."

Supreme Saint Nasia spoke again, "We are here to welcome these dear people into our family. The first thing we do in The Family of Saints is give each of you a new title. At birth, you were given a name by your parents, who were tainted by the ways of society. We give those that become a part of our family a designation to identify you as one of the family. We label you as a Saint initially, though there are other levels you can achieve, which provide additional privileges as well as responsibilities. Being a member of The Family of Saints requires cooperation, hard work and commitment, which we reward with promotions. So, please keep that in mind."

Each new inductee was asked to stand and be decreed a Saint. When Neveah stood, Supreme Saint Akadeus focused on her. Neveah watched his eyes to see if they would turn brown, triggering her disappearance like the man earlier. Instead, as Supreme Saint Nasia decreed her Saint Neveah, the man's eyes turned blue. As Neveah took her seat and wondered what that meant.

CHAPTER 27

Morning sickness settled into Neveah's pregnancy suddenly after a few days with The Family of Saints. As they'd been told, everyone had to contribute to the operation of the community as a way to pay for all that was available to them. Neveah's assignment was to work with the children. She loved working with the youngsters, but the demands of the pregnancy, along with the work was causing Neveah extreme fatigue. She figured she probably needed to get some prenatal care, but didn't know if any was available.

She'd made friends with Niecy, one of the girls in her building, who she'd found out was running away from an arrest warrant. She'd begged Neveah not to tell for fear they would kick her out of The Family. Neveah promised not to tell and would instead be her confidante. Since she'd been there longer than Neveah, Niecy was the ideal person to get information about receiving medical care.

Neveah walked through the building's common area, but didn't notice Niecy there. She went to her apartment and noticed the door was slightly ajar. Neveah knocked and the door swung open allowing her to see into the apartment. She entered and noticed the bedroom door was cracked. Neveah wondered whether she should leave the apartment altogether. It was, after all, someone else's abode.

"Niecy, are you here?"

"Just a minute," Niecy said.

A minute later, a man came out of Niecy's bedroom. When his eyes met Neveah's, he quickly diverted them. He nodded his head quickly at her as he exited the apartment. Minutes later, Niecy came out attempting to smooth her messy hair.

"So, what was that about?" Neveah asked her new friend. "I didn't think we were allowed to have visitors from the outside."

"He's not an outside visitor. He's my husband-mate."

"Husband-mate? What does that mean?"

"You don't have one yet? Every woman here gets a husband-mate to take care of whatever she needs. And I do mean whatever. You know what I'm saying?"

"I'm so confused."

"Trust me, it's a wonderful thing. I'm surprised you haven't picked one out yet."

"I don't want a husband-mate. I just want a safe place to live for me and… Anyway, I came over here to ask you about medical care. If someone needs a doctor, what do they do? Are there doctors in the camp?"

"Are you sick?"

"I'm not really sick, but I do need some medical attention."

"You need to talk to your escort. He'll help you."

"Thank you. Hey, I'm sorry I barged into your apartment. I won't do that again."

"It's okay. I should've made sure the door was closed. I hope you feel better and start thinking about what you want in a man. I'm sure they'll set up your selection soon."

Neveah left Niecy's apartment and headed back to her own. She knew there were some weird rules in place here but no one had warned her about a husband-mate. There was enough on her plate with her pregnancy, let alone adding a stranger to the mix. However, since The Family of Saints was providing a place for her to stay and food to eat, she would go along with their way of doing things even if she didn't want to.

CHAPTER 28

Niecy was correct when she told Neveah her husband-mate selection would be soon. The next day, Ellis told her it would be held two days later. Neveah dressed in the items she'd been given for the occasion and was escorted to the clearing to see how the whole process would work.

Neveah had spent time thinking about having a husband-mate. Would this selection precede marriage? Would they be dating or engaged? What if she chose someone, then found out she didn't like him? Could she choose again or maybe even decline participating in the process altogether? She looked for Niecy to ask her, but hadn't been able to find her. She would just have to see how things went.

The Chief and Assistant Chief arrived to music and cheering from the crowd and took their seats. Neveah and five other women were seated in chairs. Then, ten men appeared and lined up in front of the ladies. Neveah looked at the men and noticed they were all extremely handsome. Their skin tones ranged from pale to dark and their heights and builds had a similar range.

Akadeus' intense gaze moved across the row of women sitting in front of him. "Good afternoon. This is your husband-mate selection process," he said.

Nasia continued. "You ladies are blessed to be in The Family of Saints. Every woman here is to be treated as a queen. In order to achieve that, you each will get a husband-mate. You will each pick a man to serve you. He will replace your escorts from here on out. Each of you is a queen and whichever man you choose will be expected to fulfill every need you have. Here in the Family of Saints, women don't serve men. Men serve women. Each of these men has been thoroughly evaluated to ensure they will be good husband-mates. They are physically, mentally, and emotionally ready to serve. So, you can choose with confidence, knowing that these are good men."

When Neveah's turn came, she looked at the men and noticed one of them was mouthing, *Pick me. Pick me.* She wondered why he was so desperate for her to select him. She opened her mouth to do so, but Akadeus interrupted.

"Saint Neveah, where are you from?"

"I'm from Pontiac, Michigan."

"Why?" Nasia asked her husband.

"Because I'm going to select for her."

"You know that's not how this works. Queens get to choose their own husband-mate."

Akadeus ignored Nasia's objections and turned his attention back to Neveah. "Do you mind if I choose for you?"

"Don't let him intimidate you. Choose whomever pleases you," Nasia said, pointing at Neveah.

Neveah shrugged her shoulders. "I don't know who to select anyway, so go right ahead."

"Do I need to remind you who I am, Akadeus?" Nasia said as she swiveled her neck. "I'll tell you. I'm the leader of this here organization."

"I know you're the leader but do you remember who I am?"

"Go ahead and tell me who you are."

"I'm god and I select Art."

Neveah realized Akadeus must indeed be God, because he selected the man who'd been silently pleading with her to select him. How would he have known if he wasn't God?

***

Neveah walked briskly from the ceremony with her husband-mate, Art, close behind her. All she could think about was Akadeus' statement that he was god.

"I knew this wasn't a good idea," Neveah mumbled as she headed toward her room.

"Hold up," Art said breathlessly.

Neveah stopped abruptly and turned to face the man. With her hands on her hips she yelled, "Why are you following me?"

The man stopped just short of running into Neveah. "I'm trying to get to know you and ..." he turned to see who was around that might hear him. Seeing no one, he whispered, "I need to talk to you privately. I've been sent to help you."

"Yeah, yeah. I know. It's your job because you're my husband-mate."

"No, I mean I've been *sent*."

"What are you saying?"

"I've been sent by God to help you."

"I know. I was there, remember?"

"You don't understand."

"Well, I don't plan to get an understanding in my apartment, so stop following me."

"Okay, I won't come with you."

"Thank you." Neveah stomped off toward her apartment, confused about what she'd gotten herself into. Her husband-mate was already getting on her nerves. And what did he mean when he said he was sent by God anyway?

CHAPTER 29

Neveah stepped away from her stove to see who was banging on her door, as if she didn't know. Art had been there no less than three times a day for the last few days, trying to get into her apartment. She looked through the peephole to confirm her suspicions.

"I know you see me. If I have to, I'll come every day until you let me in."

Neveah leaned back on the door and exhaled loudly. She was tired of avoiding Art but at the same time, she didn't want anything to do with a husband-mate, regardless of who it was. She decided she would hear what he had to say and be done with it. Perhaps they could both move on afterward.

She opened the door and stared at her husband-mate. He really was quite handsome, in a schoolboy kind of way. Neveah loved his curly, brownish-red hair and puckered lips. If the situations were different, she might allow herself to entertain the possibilities with Art. However, she had much more to deal with than romance.

The two stood looking at each other. Neveah stepped back from the door and gestured for Art to enter.

"Are you really letting me in?" he asked, swiftly entering the space before Neveah could change her mind.

"Just have a seat so we can get this over with."

Art fell onto Neveah's couch and she did as well.

"Nice place. Terrible attitude. What gives?"

"I just don't like this whole husband-mate thing. I'm not interested in a romantic relationship right now and it seems I don't have much of a choice around here."

"Who said this is a romantic relationship?"

"Isn't it? Niecy and her husband-mate are... involved." Neveah paused a beat. "Wait a minute. Is this some sort of prostitution ring or something? I can't believe this!" Neveah slapped her hand on her forehead. "I have to get out of here, but where will I go?"

Art stood and lightly touched Neveah's arm. "No, that's not what this is at all. I'm here only to do what you need. Nothing more."

"But why, Art? This makes no sense," Neveah said, standing and pacing in front of the couch.

"I got myself into something I haven't been able to get out of but this is not about prostitution."

Neveah pondered what Art said. Husband-mates were supposed to serve the women they were assigned to and she didn't want what Niecy did from her husband-mate, so maybe she didn't have to leave.

"Look, I think you're a nice guy and all, but this arrangement isn't going to work for me. I'll just tell them I don't want a husband-mate and they'll probably put you back in the pool or something, so someone else can select you."

Art's eyes bulged as he rushed toward Neveah. "No, you can't do that," he said as he waved his hands. "You have to let me help you," Art frantically explained.

"But I don't want all this. I just need a safe place to live."

"If you tell them that, Nasia will think I'm not holding up my end of the bargain and there will be major repercussions."

"What repercussions? What are you talking about?"

"Trust me, you can't do that. Please. I'll do whatever you want."

"Okay! Jeez. Don't get upset. I don't want to make trouble for you, so we'll just get through this."

"Thank you. You have no idea how much I appreciate that."

CHAPTER 30

Art and Neveah developed a routine that allowed Art to stay in the Pooles' good graces, but yet allowed Neveah the space she desired. Art's desire was to get to know Neveah better. The young woman caused something to rise up within him that he hadn't felt in a very long time. He didn't just want to be her husband-mate, she inspired him to go above and beyond those duties.

He knocked on Neveah's door and waited for her to answer. It was her night to prepare a meal and it was dinner time.

Neveah opened the door and immediately returned to the kitchen.

"Come on in," she said, opening the door then moving away.

Art watched as her full curly head of hair bounced as she rushed to the kitchen. He desired to touch her hair, to feel its softness. However, he felt she might see him as being too forward if he did, so he resisted.

"I need to take these fries out before they burn." Neveah pulled the basket from the fryer and tossed the fries onto a paper towel covered plate then salted the fried potatoes. "How are you?"

"I'm good. How has your day been?"

"It's been okay." Neveah yawned.

"Didn't get enough sleep last night?"

"The children were a little energetic today for some reason, so I'm a little tired. That's all."

Art came to Neveah's side. "Why don't you rest while I finish cooking the burgers."

"Next time. Thank you for offering, though."

She moved about the kitchen melting cheese on their burgers, placing lettuce, tomatoes and pickles on a plate, and setting out condiments.

Art got two glasses from the cabinets and poured grape Kool-Aid in each of them. He sat at the table as Neveah placed the last plate on the table. Each of them prepared their burgers as they liked, placed fries and their plates and began to eat.

"Wow! What did you do to these burgers? They are great!" Art asked, covering his mouth as he spoke and chewed.

Neveah giggled. "I didn't do anything special." She popped a couple of fries in her mouth.

"You're being modest. They are terrific." He wiped his mouth with a napkin and pinned Neveah's eyes with his. She smiled and gazed into his as well. "I don't believe you've ever mentioned your family. Tell me about your parents."

Neveah's demeanor changed at the mention of her family. Art wondered if perhaps he shouldn't have mentioned it. It was too late. The words had already escaped his lips, so he allowed the request to linger in the air.

Neveah cleared her throat. "I don't know where either of my parents are right now. I thought my father was dead, but my mother told me he was alive not too long ago."

"Where do you think they are?"

"My mother is either in jail or dead for killing my stepfather. I have no idea where my father is."

"I'm sorry," Art sympathized with the young woman. He touched her hand and continued. "That's got to be tough."

Neveah nodded before taking her empty plate to the kitchen, placing it in the dishwater and washing it.

"What about your family?"

"There's not much to tell. My father was an alcoholic. He died when I was twelve in a drunk driving accident. For some reason, my mother blamed me for his death and she finally kicked me out of the house at fourteen. I haven't had much contact with her since then." He'd fought hard but his voice began to break and a few tears fell. "I used to go past the house every now and then, until I saw new people living there. I don't know where she is."

Neveah returned to the table and wiped a stray tear away from Art's face, then stood behind his chair and hugged him as he cried softly.

CHAPTER 31

Neveah went across the hall to Niecy's apartment and knocked on her door. While she did enjoy spending time with Art, she also yearned for some girl time as well.

"Hey girl. Come on in," Niecy said, stepping aside to allow Neveah entry.

The two got comfortable in the living room as soft music played in the background.

"I was surprised when you said you wanted to hang out tonight. You're usually busy with Art."

"Well, I needed some girl time. Is that okay?"

"That's okay, but what about you and your fine husband-mate, Art?"

"What about him?"

"He's trying to be more than a husband-mate, honey." Niecy placed her foot on the table in front of her chair.

"No, he's not," Neveah lied. She was aware of Art's interest in her and she had some interest in him as well. Neither had verbally expressed it yet. However, she didn't want to discuss Art tonight. She just wanted to hang out and enjoy some girl talk.

"Husband-mates don't have dinner with the women they serve every night and they don't look at them the way Art looks at you. Girl, that man looks like you're a bowl of gravy he just can't wait to sop up. Husband-mates just do what they're asked and that's it."

"I don't know about all of that. He's just a nice guy."

"Yeah okay. People that were at your husband-mate selection said he begged you to pick him as your husband-mate. Did he?"

"I won't confirm nor deny that."

Niecy laughed. "You just did."

Suddenly, a loud horn sounded. Niecy leapt from her seat.

"We have to go," Niecy said, grabbing Neveah by the hand and pulling her up.

Neveah followed Niecy as she rushed toward the clearing. When they arrived, Akadeus and Nasia were mounting their seats.

Once the crowd got quiet, Akadeus spoke. "Saints of The Family of Saints, I want to be sure everyone, new or seasoned, knows what is allowed here. I heard there is at least one Bible being passed around in this compound. Bibles and other Christian paraphernalia are strictly prohibited. If you believe in that fantasy then I encourage you to just leave. If we find out who is responsible, they will be severely punished."

The crowd buzzed as Nasia and Akadeus climbed down from their perches and returned to their home. Neveah approached Art to ask him about the announcement. However, Art slightly shook his head and walked away, leaving Neveah confused. *Did Art give me a Bible and not let me know it was against the rules to have it here?*

Later, a knock at the door summoned Neveah out of her nap to answer it.

"Who is it?" she asked, waiting for an answer.

"It's me," Art said.

Neveah let Art in and returned to the couch with Art following.

"Why didn't you tell me this wasn't allowed?" Neveah asked, pulling the Bible from under the sofa cushion. "You could've gotten me in trouble."

Art exhaled then focused on Neveah. "I'm sorry I didn't think of that. I didn't tell you because I didn't want you to be comfortable with it and not afraid to have it."

"Are you responsible for the Bibles Akadeus was talking about?"

Art nodded. "People need hope and the Bibles give them that."

"But what if you get caught?"

"I have to take the risk. It's that important," Art said, taking Neveah's hand in his. "Don't let that concern you. I'll be okay."

"But, I am concerned. I care about you," Neveah's voice cracked, communicating the fear she felt.

Art smiled. "I didn't know you cared about me beyond this whole husband-mate relationship."

"I didn't realize it until recently myself, but I do care about you a lot. Please be careful. I really don't want you to get hurt."

"I'm not going to do anything that will keep me away from you."

What is God's Name

Neveah felt calm after Art's reassurance and smiled at him as the two stared into each other's eyes.

CHAPTER 32

Art and Neveah went for a walk in the woods surrounding the Family of Saints' compound. Neveah had never gone past the clearing though Art had been trying to get her to explore the other parts of the grounds for days. Neveah always had one excuse or another, but finally agreed to the branch out a little and see more of the property. The landscape was scenic with trails winding through thick woods and along the shores of small inland lakes and ponds. Art reached for Neveah's hand and she allowed him to grasp it.

In a clearing that opened up to a pond, Art led her to one of the benches situated there.

"I didn't even know all of this was out here. It's beautiful!"

"That's because you refused to leave your safety zone. Have a seat," Art said as Neveah sat on the bench, curious about the true purpose for the walk.

"Water is so soothing. Whenever I get stressed out or anxious about anything, I love to find some water to settle myself down."

"I feel the same way." Art focused on the horizon where the sun was beginning to set.

They each soaked up the peacefulness they were experiencing in the moment. Neveah removed her sandals, walked over to the shore's edge, and dipped her toes in the water. She leapt, kicking her legs out, eliciting a chuckle from herself and Art.

"I feel so free. I'm glad I agreed to venture out a little today."

"See, I told you."

Neveah returned to the bench. She scooted close to Art and allowed her head to rest on his shoulder, surprising even herself. Art followed her lead and took her hand once again.

"I've been thinking about something you told me," Neveah spoke.

"What is that?"

"You told me God sent you. What did you mean by that?"

Art sat stoically for a few moments as though he was trying to figure out how to answer Neveah's question.

"Sometime before you arrived, I knew in my heart someone would be coming into my life that God wanted me to help. You even showed up in my dreams. When I saw you that day at the husband-mate selection, I knew you were that person. I believe God caused our paths to cross for a reason."

"Really? How do you know it's me? I mean, it could be anybody."

"I can't explain it but I just know. Don't you feel a connection between us?"

"I do, but not romantically."

"Says the girl with her head resting on my shoulder and her hand in mine."

Neveah lifted her head slightly and smiled at the man who smiled back at her. She loved his smile. Something about it lit up her world. She felt herself becoming even more fond of this man who had done so much for her since she'd arrived at the Family of Saints. His main job was to serve her, but he'd done so much more.

"What do you think is the reason for us meeting?"

"I believe God wants me to show you what His love feels like."

"Art, I haven't told you everything about me. You might change your mind if you knew. You haven't asked me, but I know you can see I'm pregnant."

"I already know some of it."

"You need to know how this happened. I was constantly raped by my stepfather and that's how my baby was conceived. You don't want a woman like me, Art. I'm tainted. I'm damaged because of all that I've been through. I don't know how God could even love someone like me."

"None of that impacts His love. He doesn't love us based on what we've been through or even what we've done. He loves you without even taking any of that into account. You are not what you've been through. God knows all of that and He still loves you."

"How could God love me and yet let me go through all that I've experienced?"

"I can't tell you why you've gone through what you have. I do know God's love is unconditional and there is purpose in everything that happens in our lives. God could have interrupted the things that happened to you. But He doesn't make people do what He wants. He can't go against His own rules. God does touch the hearts and minds of people, but the ultimate decision about their behavior is theirs."

"What about you, Art? How do you feel about me, knowing I'm messed up because of my past?"

Art directed Neveah's head from his shoulder with his index finger and focused his eyes on hers. He lowered his lips to her forehead.

"Neveah, I know I'm supposed to just be your husband-mate, but I've come to care more deeply about you. Sometimes our scars make us beautiful and attractive, even when we don't feel that way about ourselves. Let me show you God's love."

"You really think God loves me?"

"God is love. It's who He is. He can't help Himself and He's not trying to and it doesn't depend on you. It is solely about who He is."

"How do I let you and God love me?"

"One of the ways we experience God's love is through other people. You have a wall up around your heart to protect yourself from being hurt. You're serving a self-imposed sentence in a prison you built. Let those walls fall flat. Trust that God is not out to hurt you. Know that I have no intention to do anything to harm you, either. That doesn't mean you won't get hurt, but know if something like that does happen, it's not because I'm trying to hurt you. It's just a sign of my humanity."

"I don't know if I can do that. You're right. I've put a guard up to protect myself for so long."

"Has your wall kept you from being hurt?"

Neveah paused for a couple of beats before shaking her head. "No, it hasn't."

"Try something different, then. I promise you won't regret it."

"Alright, Art. I'll try. But remember, this is new to me so you'll need to have patience."

They sat a while longer, soaking in the scenery, thinking about the conversation they'd shared and enjoying one another's presence.

"One of the little girls I work with has been telling me her mother's husband-mate has been touching her."

"Who is it?"

"I can't tell you because I would be betraying her confidence. I've been telling her she should tell her mother, but I think she's afraid of how her mother will respond or if she'll even believe her."

"Neveah, you can't let this continue, waiting on a little girl to get up the nerve to tell her mother. You might have to tell her mother yourself."

"You think so?"

"I do."

"Could this be the reason I went through what I did? So, I can help others who have gone through this?"

"It could be. I'm sure the conversations you two had has been helpful to her. Sometimes, people just need to know they're not alone. But you have a responsibility to make sure her mother knows what her husband-mate is doing. If her mother won't listen, you need to speak to Akadeus and Nasia about it directly.

Some things might not go the way they should around here, but I promise you they'll take care of this issue."

CHAPTER 33

Neveah and Khloe's mother, Chivonne, went out to the lake to talk. Neveah had extended the invitation after her conversation with Art the day before. She felt it was necessary to move as quickly as possible in an attempt to spare Khloe all of the pain she could.

"I'm sure you're wondering why I asked you to come out here with me."

"I assume it's about Khloe since you work with her in school."

"That's exactly what I want talk about."

The two arrived at the lake Art had shown to Neveah. Since that time, Neveah had found herself out here a few times because of the peacefulness the water gave her.

"Have a seat, please."

After sitting, Chivonne began. "Is Khloe having a problem in school?"

"No, she's doing very well in her studies. The teacher actually has her helping others when she's done with her work, so that's not a problem."

"Well, what is it, then?"

"Your daughter confided something in me I think you should know. I haven't shared it with anyone else. I felt I should bring it to you first."

"Okay, I'm listening."

"Your daughter told me your husband-mate has been molesting her."

The girl's mother drew and released a deep breath.

"She told you about that?" Chivonne asked.

"Yes, she did."

"I'm surprised she told you. She was very hesitant to tell me."

"Oh, so you knew?" Neveah couldn't believe Chivonne knew what her daughter was dealing with and did nothing to stop it.

"I did." Chivonne allowed her gaze to travel over the lake.

"Have you told Chief Saint Akadeaus or Nasia about this?"

"I'm afraid to because my husband-mate is a trusted advisor. I don't know if they'll believe me if I told them."

"But what about your daughter? You have to protect her."

"I know and I'm doing that by not letting her be alone with him. However, sometimes it can't be helped. I don't know what to do."

"I'm telling you every time he touches her inappropriately, it affects her. She knows you know, yet she still has to endure the violation. Khloe needs to know she can trust you to protect her and based on what you said, she can't depend on you for that."

Chivonne gave Neveah the side-eye. "How old are you, huh? You can't be much older than my daughter," Chivonne asked, her attitude apparent.

"I'm eighteen."

"I'm trying to figure out what qualifies you to tell me what I should be doing?"

"Ma'am, I may be young, but I've experienced a lot and I'm familiar with how stuff like this can affect a person."

"Listen, I am a grown woman and this is my child. Not yours. You have no idea what you're talking about."

Neveah rubbed her round belly as she contemplated how she would respond to Chivonne's comment. "My mother married a man who appeared to be a nice guy. I enjoyed having a father in the home since I never knew my own. He bought me all kinds of things and took me to the movies and stuff. I loved him and couldn't wait for him to be my daddy. Shortly after he moved in, things changed. My mother worked nights, so I would be alone with Otis. Every night my mother went to work, my stepfather would force me to have sex with him. He trained me to please him. That's not something a child should experience. And this child I'm carrying? It's my stepfather's."

Chivonne lowered her head. "I'm sorry. I didn't know."

"It's a part of my life I don't talk about. I couldn't help but think about it when your daughter told me what she was going through."

"I'm sorry I came at you like that. Maybe you're not blaming me like I thought you were. I see you're trying to help my daughter. I still don't know how much more I can do to protect her." Chivonne dropped her head into her hands and broke down crying. "Akadeus and Nasia aren't going to believe me because of their relationship with my husband-mate."

"Maybe they'll believe me."

Chivonne raised her head to look at Neveah. "You would do that?"

"Without a doubt. There's a young lady's life and well-being at risk."

"You don't want to get involved in this. You could find yourself in a world of trouble. Trust me. Let's just think about this a little more. Maybe there's another way."

"What other choice do we have? This has to end for your daughter's sake. I'm not afraid. I believe God will take care of me."

***

Neveah and Chivonne carried on a light conversation as they walked back to the compound. During their silent moments, Neveah thought about what she was planning to do. She wondered if she should have been so quick to volunteer to get involved. On the other hand, Khloe's plight was so similar to her own, it gave Neveah extra incentive to help out in any way she could.

She decided to go in search for Art. She needed him to tell her she was doing the right thing by volunteering to help Khloe escape the abuse she was experiencing in her own home. She and Khloe's mother separated when they got back to camp. The clearing was full of people, so Neveah decided to look around to see if Art was there. She stopped and spoke to several people before hearing Art's distinctive laughter. She followed the sound and located her husband-mate with a group of other husband-mates. Seeming to sense her presence, his eyes met hers before she even got close to him.

Neveah saw his smile widen and his adoration for her in his eyes became even more evident than it typically was. His love for her was confirmed once again. Her love for him was a huge discovery for her.

As she approached him, he excused himself from the conversation to meet her. He opened his arms and once she was close enough, she fell into them. She smiled as she realized she'd finally found the security and love she'd been searching for, in the arms of her husband-mate in a group called The Family of Saints. Neveah could only shake her head at the irony of it all.

"How are you?" Art asked, kissing Neveah on the top of her head.

"I'm fine. I know you're doing okay, standing around here talking and laughing with everyone."

"I feel pretty good. How did things go?"

"That's what I wanted to talk to you about."

"Do we need to go to your place so we can have some privacy?"

"Yes, if you don't mind leaving."

"Anything for you. Let's go."

Neveah and Art walked hand in hand to Neveah's apartment. Once inside, Neveah gestured for Art to sit on the couch.

"Do you want something to drink or snack on?"

"Is this serious? Come sit down next to me," Art patted the couch cushion next to him. "Tell me what's going on."

"I spoke to Khloe's mother about what her daughter told me."

"How did she take it?"

"She already knew about it. She's afraid to tell Akadeus and Nasia about it because her husband-mate is close to them. She doesn't think they'll believe her."

"So, she's not going to say anything?"

"No, she's not. I'm going to report him to the Pooles."

"You're going to do what?"

"I can't know about this and not say anything!"

"What if she's not telling the truth? You'll be hanging out there by yourself."

"You think she's lying?"

"I don't know. But what I do know is her own mother won't stand up for her, and clearly, that's her job."

"That's because she's afraid of how Akadeus and Nasia will react, Art. Not because she doesn't believe her daughter."

"What if they don't believe you? Do you know how mean they can be? There's no telling how they'll punish you if they think you deserve it and don't forget you're carrying a child."

Neveah processed what Art was saying. She wasn't afraid for herself but she wasn't sure if it was smart to put herself in a position to possibly endure a physical punishment especially considering her pregnancy. The baby took that moment to kick Neveah, causing her breath to catch in her throat. Neveah looked down as the baby rolled from one side of her belly to the other. Once the child had settled down, she smiled and looked up at Art who smiled in return.

"If I didn't know better, I would say my baby was trying to tell me to do this."

"Is there anything I can do to talk you out of this?"

"I don't think so. This reminds me of the story of Esther we talked about. I believe I was born to do this. Just like Esther, I'll be just fine and so will my baby."

"There's no way I'm going to let you do this alone. I'll be there with you. Actually, I'll tell them what's going on. At least that way if there's any backlash, maybe I'll take the brunt of it so you and the baby will be safer. Trust me on this."

"I really think I should be doing this but I'll follow your lead."

CHAPTER 34

The next day, Art and Neveah headed to speak with Supreme Saints Akadeus and Nasia. They had talked about their plan for presenting the issue. They knew who would say what and how they would say it. They had carefully choreographed the encounter to achieve their desired outcome...dealing with Chivonne's husband-mate's behavior.

When they arrived at the Pooles' home, they were ushered into a space which served as a conference room for necessary meetings. Shortly thereafter, the leaders of The Family of Saints entered the room.

Neveah looked at Akadeus to see what color his eyes were and they hadn't changed colors...yet. She assumed this was a good sign and released the breath she was holding. She thought, *maybe this won't be so bad.*

"Y'all said it was an emergency and you needed to speak with us. What is it? I want to get back to what I was doing." Nasia's attitude was obvious. It was clear she was the one to watch during this meeting.

"There's something going on we think you should know about. A young lady reported being molested by a man here in The Family of Saints. We feel you should know so he can be dealt with accordingly. We're sure you would agree with us," Art stated, looking between Akadeus and Nasia.

Akadeus shot up from his seat, a scowl settling on his face. "Who is it?" Akadeus' voice boomed in response to hearing the allegation.

Neveah watched as his eyes turned to red.

"It's Cleveland. Chivonne's husband-mate," Art responded.

Nasia scooted to the edge of her chair as if she had to move closer to hear. "Are you saying Khloe accused Cleveland of molesting her?"

"Yes, we are," Neveah chimed in. "Khloe told me about it directly."

"I don't believe her. Cleveland just isn't that type of person," Nasia explained. "He wouldn't do something like that."

"Nasia, I believe Khloe. She has no reason to lie. I..."

"Supreme Saint Nasia to you!"

"Ladies, calm down," Akadeus brought the heated exchange to a halt. He then turned his attention to Art and Neveah. "What you're saying is very serious and hard to believe. Like Nasia said, Cleveland is not the kind of man who would act inappropriately with a child. Somebody had better have some proof."

Akadeus looked between Art and Neveah. Neveah glanced at Art, hoping he would know what to say in that moment.

"We don't have any proof other than the child's word," Art said.

"Well, let's talk to her. Hey!" He snapped his fingers and two men came in the room and stood at attention. "We're going out to the clearing. Get Khloe and bring her there. We might as well get Cleveland, too."

The men rushed from the room to complete their assignment.

Fifteen minutes later, a buzz rose up as it seemed everyone in The Family of Saints had gathered to witness what was going to happen in the clearing. Neveah and Art stood amongst the crowd waiting for Khloe to be brought out.

Neveah felt a tap on her shoulder, causing her to turn around and look into Chivonne's angry eyes.

"I hope you're happy."

Seconds later, Khloe was dragged into the middle of the clearing. The teen fought to free herself from the men who had her by the arms. When that didn't work, she dug her feet into the dirt, attempting to stop the movement. The teary-eyed young woman looked into the crowd for her mother. When their eyes locked, she called out to her for help. When her eyes landed on Neveah's, her anger and disappointment were obvious. Neveah believed Khloe was angry at her for causing all of this to happen. Hopefully, she would realize Neveah did this for her own good.

Once the girl reached a spot directly in front of Nasia and Akadeus' thrones, the men stopped dragging her. Instead, they held her in place to keep her from leaving.

"Saint Khloe, we've been told something terrible has been happening to you here in our compound. Do you know what I'm referring to?"

Khloe shook her head in response as Cleveland was being led into the clearing.

"We'll fill you in. Saint Neveah and Husband-mate Art said Cleveland was exhibiting inappropriate behavior with you. Now do you know what we're talking about?"

Khloe jumped as Cleveland wrestled with the men holding him. "I didn't do anything to that girl. I don't know why she's lying."

Flashbacks of Otis' denial caused Neveah to react before she could think. She ran over to Cleveland and yelled, "How could you stand here and lie like this?" Just as Neveah raised her hand to strike him, Art grabbed her hand to prevent her from doing so.

"I know you're upset but you don't want to do that," he whispered. "That'll just cause more problems," he said as he led Neveah away from the man desperately trying to escape the grasp of the men restricting his movement.

"Khloe, we're waiting for your answer. Is there any truth to what we've been told?"

The fright evident on Khloe's face broke Neveah's heart. She knew exactly what the young lady was feeling, being exposed in such a manner in front of the person who violated her. Neveah wished she'd gone about this in a way that would've spared such a spectacle. However, there was no way she could've predicted exactly how Nasia and Akadeus would handle things. All she could hope was this wouldn't add additional angst for Khloe and ultimately, changes would take place in her home to alleviate any further abuse.

"Cleveland didn't do anything inappropriate. He's been a great husband-mate for my mother," Khloe whispered. "I don't know where Neveah got that information from."

"Khloe, no one said anything about where we got the information from. How did you know it was Neveah?" Nasia mentioned.

Khloe dropped her head, refusing to look at anyone, including Nasia and Akadeus. Her silence in response to being caught in a lie was deafening. Her sobs rose above the buzz of those standing around the clearing as it became obvious she was having an emotional breakdown. Chivonne rushed to her daughter's side and the two gripped each other as though releasing the other would have dire consequences.

Nasia focused on the hugging mother and daughter, along with Cleveland, who was sweating as a result of his struggles to free himself.

"Bring Cleveland closer to me," Nasia said, glaring at the suspected molester.

When Cleveland was standing at the Nasia's feet, she spoke. "Cleveland, you have been a trusted friend and advisor of The Family of Saints and we love you. It grieves me to hear these allegations against you and it hurts even more to realize the truth of them. Take him away. We'll deal with him later." Nasia turned her head as Cleveland was being taken away.

"Wait!" Akadeus' voice rose above the noise of the crowd, causing everyone's attention to turn toward him. "Bring him back."

Everyone waited until Cleveland stood before Akadeus.

"I don't believe Khloe ever said Cleveland did what he was accused of. I'm going to give her another chance to tell me whether the allegations are true or not." Akadeus waited for a few moments to allow Khloe to respond one way or the other.

Khloe fell to the ground at her mother's feet as her breakdown continued.

Chivonne knelt next her daughter. "Please just leave her alone. She's already been through enough."

"Khloe is unwilling to confirm it. Release him," Akadeus demanded, prompting the men to follow his direction. Cleveland ran from the clearing and disappeared from everyone's sight.

"I knew you would never believe that Cleveland did this to my daughter," Chivonne yelled. "I'm taking my daughter and leaving this place. I should've done it a long time ago. Maybe my daughter wouldn't have had to endure what she has."

Chivonne pulled Khloe from the ground and led her away from the clearing.

"How can you just overrule me, Akadeus? I already pronounced Cleveland guilty and you openly went against me."

"I'm god and I know things you don't," Akadeus responded.

"You're not God," Neveah said.

Art whispered to Neveah, "You can't say that. Akadeus doesn't take too kindly to anyone challenging his proclamation that he's god."

"What did you say?" Akadeus roared.

Neveah realized she had accidently let her beliefs slip from her lips.

"Um, what do you think I said?"

"You don't ask us questions, Neveah. Now answer him," Nasia demanded.

"I'm not going to lie. I said you aren't God."

Akadeus leaned forward with his eyebrows kissing each other in the center of his forehead.

"Who is God, then?"

"He is the God of the Bible."

"And where did you get that idea from?"

"The Bible," Neveah whispered.

"Where did you get the Bible from?"

Neveah refused to respond.

"Answer me!" The intensity with which Akadeus yelled caused his body to vibrate.

"I won't."

"We don't allow the Bible in the Family of Saints. It's a fairytale and gives people false hope about a savior that has no power, if He even exists. I'm going to ask you one more time where you got the Bible. Did you bring it with you when you came here?"

"No, I did not and I won't say where I got it from."

"I'm going to give you a chance to renounce this God you speak of and recognize me as god. That God doesn't exist. Only me."

Art spoke up, sparing Neveah from having to respond. "We won't renounce the true and living God."

"Then you must be willing to take the punishment for your offenses," Nasia declared.

"God help us," Art whispered, gripping Neveah's hand.

A few of the men gathered around Art and Neveah, waiting

for instructions as to what to do next.

"You have broken two of our major rules and you will be punished severely. Your sentence will be..." Nasia started.

"We're isolating the two of you from The Family. Your sentence will be to live outside of the camp in the wilderness for three nights with no food, water, or shelter." Akadeus interrupted Nasia before she could complete her sentence.

"That's not tough enough, Akadeus. You can't let them get away with a light punishment, because others will see that and challenge us."

"What about my baby?" Neveah yelled. "Please, my baby didn't have anything to do with this."

"Since I'm not God, let your God take care of you and your baby out there. Take them away," Akadeus instructed.

The men led a weeping Neveah and a praying Art through the wooded area surrounding the compound. When they arrived at a ten-foot tall fence with a gate in the middle of it, the men unlocked the gate, pushed the couple through it, relocked it and walked away.

CHAPTER 35

Neveah snoozed as the sun disappeared behind the trees and the sounds of nature got louder. She had sobbed until she fell asleep, despite Art reminding her of how stress could affect the health of her baby. Art stroked Neveah's hair as he watched a fox scamper by in the distance, stopping to stare at the couple for a moment then continuing on its way. Though Art told her not to worry, he was concerned about their well-being in the woods without the comforts of The Family of Saints compound.

He had known Akadeus and Nasia for years and couldn't believe they would treat them so cruelly. He'd seen punishment meted out to others that was worse, but considering Neveah was a young pregnant woman and he was a long-time friend, he thought a little leniency would have been in order. However, he was apparently wrong, which strengthened his resolve to get out of the group. He knew it would be challenging to do so, but he had to at least try.

He looked at the woman laying her head across his lap and knew he had to protect her. Not only because she was carrying precious cargo, she was also precious cargo herself. He would do whatever was necessary because of how deeply he cared for her. Though his job was to serve her within the confines of The Family of Saints, his feelings went much further...more than he even imagined they would.

Neveah stirred and opened her eyes. He looked deep into them as they acclimated to the environment. She stretched then abruptly sat up. Immediately, the tears began to flow.

"Hey, did you sleep well?"

"No, I didn't." Neveah rubbed her arms. "It's cold, too."

"Yeah, the sun is going down."

"Art, I don't think I can do this. Do you think I can change my mind and tell them I don't believe in God?"

"Don't think like that. Besides, who would you tell? I don't expect them to come back until they're ready to let us back in."

Neveah panicked. "What are we going to do? What are we going to eat?"

"Remember I told you God is always with us?"

"Yes."

"He's with us even sitting in the middle of this forest and I don't believe He's going to let us down. He'll come through for us. It might be tough, but we'll make it through."

The two heard movement on the other side of the fence.

"Did you hear that?" Neveah asked, running toward the gate.

"Yes, I did," Art joined her at the fence. "Who's there?"

The sound of someone fiddling with the lock confirmed there was someone there. Neveah and Art heard the sound of the lock being pulled from the latch and saw the gate's handle move. When the gate opened, Akadeus appeared.

"What are you doing out here, Akadeus? Are you here to tease us or punish us further?" Art sarcastically spoke to his friend.

"I deserve that, but I came to rescue you."

"Why did you send us out here in the first place?" Neveah asked.

"If I hadn't, Nasia would've come up with a punishment that could've been much more detrimental to the two of you and I wasn't going to have my…" Akadeus eyed Neveah, causing her to feel somewhat nervous. "I couldn't let that happen. Here's what we're going to do. I'm going to sneak the two of you back into Neveah's apartment. No one can know you're there so you'll have to stay in the apartment until your punishment is over."

"Why are you doing this? I mean, you send us out here then you let us off. I'm just curious," Neveah wondered aloud.

"Either follow me or don't," Akadeus said as he lit the lantern he had in his hand. "Come on."

Neveah and Art followed Akadeus closely. Art held Neveah's hand to help stabilize her movement over the uneven terrain. When they got closer to the camp, Akadeus led them around the wooded edge of the clearing and into the building where Neveah's apartment was. Once inside, Neveah and Art relaxed and smiled. God had indeed taken care of them and they were thankful for it.

CHAPTER 36

With their sentence complete and their existence in The Family of Saints back to normal, Neveah and Art's relationship continued to grow and mature. The time they'd spent hidden in Neveah's apartment brought about a stronger bond they both found enjoyable and they each desired it to be strengthened even more.

Art rushed into Neveah's apartment, nervously looking over his shoulder.

"Close the door," Art said, helping Neveah do so.

"What is going on?" Neveah wondered.

"Listen, I got some information for you, but I need you to keep it to yourself for now."

"What information?"

"I really need to know you'll keep it to yourself."

"I don't like to make promises like that when I don't know exactly what I'm agreeing to, but I guess I will."

"I've been looking into something for you and I finally found what I was looking for."

"Okay, you seem excited so I'm guessing it's good news."

"It is. Neveah, it's about your mother."

Neveah's mouth dropped open. "I didn't even know you were looking for her."

"I didn't want to get your hopes up in case I wasn't successful."

"I'm almost afraid to ask."

"Don't be afraid. Go ahead. Ask me."

"Where is she? Is she okay?"

He pulled a folded-up piece of paper from his pocket. "I'm glad you asked. She's in the Women's Huron Valley Correctional Facility in Michigan."

"Wow," Neveah said as she began pacing her living room. After all of this time, she finally had a definitive answer to her questions about her mother's well-being since she'd last seen her.

"At least she's alive. I'm thankful for that."

"I'm glad I had good news to share with you."

"I need to see her. Can you help me with that?"

"Getting you out of here and to the prison without the Pooles finding out is going to be a challenge."

"You can't tell me I can't go see her, now that I know where she is. Please. There has to be a way."

Art looked into Neveah's eyes so intently that she swore he could see into her very soul. He knew he had to make this happen for her somehow, if for no other reason than her emotional health. It would absolutely devastate her not to see her mother, even if the visit had to happen in the visitor's room of a prison. As her husband-mate, he needed to protect Neveah and provide assistance as necessary. As someone who had developed deeper feelings for her, his desire to do this for her was much greater.

"Let me see what I can do and whatever you do, don't tell anyone. I know you're going to have to fill out this visitor application and I'll make sure it gets to the prison. We'll take it from there."

Neveah took the application Art offered her and ran into his arms, hugging him tightly.

"Thank you, Art. I appreciate you," she said. She pulled away from him enough to look into his eyes. In a move that surprised them both, she pressed her lips onto his. Neither moved from their silent embrace for a few moments, comfortable in each other's arms.

"Um, wow!" Art exclaimed. "That was awesome!"

"I don't even know how that happened."

"It doesn't matter how it happened. Can we do it again?"

Neveah giggled. "No, I'll save that until after I see my mother. That'll give you a little incentive."

"You got it. Give me some time." Art rushed out of the room much like he'd rushed into it, only this time, he was on a different mission.

CHAPTER 37

Neveah had just exited the shower when she heard knocking on her apartment door. She ran her hands through her wet hair, spreading the product she'd put in it for her natural hair. The knocking persisted, causing Neveah to wrap a towel around her wet body and put her robe on over that. She slid her feet into her fluffy pink slippers on and went to the door.

Looking through the peephole, Neveah confirmed her suspicions. There was Art anxiously bouncing from one foot to the other. Just as he was turning away from the door, Neveah answered it.

Art stood looking at her as though he was in a daze. She pushed her wet curly hair back off of her forehead and ran her towel across her face.

"Sorry, I was just getting out of the shower when you knocked," she said, revealing a smile. "Come on in."

Art followed without responding.

"Are you okay?" Neveah wondered, sitting on the couch. "You haven't said a word since you've been here."

"Uh, yeah. You're just so beautiful. You take my breath away."

Neveah blushed because of Art's compliment. No other boy had ever said such kind words to her. That was because Art wasn't a boy. He was a man and his words warmed her heart and gave her a thirst to hear more of them.

"Thank you."

"Do you want me to come back so you can dry your hair and everything?"

"I usually let my hair air dry, so we're fine. What's up?"

"I have a plan to get you to the prison."

"That's great, Art! How are we going to do that?"

"It's going to be pretty easy as long as you follow my directions."

"I'm listening."

Art propped an elbow on the back of the couch. "The bus will be here tomorrow with some new people joining The Family and when it leaves, you're going to be on it."

"I'm just going to get on the bus and tell the driver where I want to go? That's not going to work!"

"Yes, it will. Let me finish. The bus driver is a husband-mate. I've already talked to him and he's agreed to take you to the prison and bring you back. We just have to make sure you get on the bus without anyone noticing."

"Okay. Go on."

"You know how everybody gathers around when new people get here?"

"Yes."

"While everyone is clapping and cheering, you make sure you're in the crowd close to the bus. Once everyone is off, you make your way onto it."

Neveah ran the scenario over in her mind. "What happens if they see me?"

"I'm going to make sure that doesn't happen. I'll be standing right there beside you. We're in this together. Just be ready to go by one o'clock."

CHAPTER 38

The next day, Art's plan worked to perfection and Neveah had arrived at the prison as planned. She really wished Art had been able to come with her, but he'd said it would've been difficult to explain his absence. He felt it was best if she went alone. He had instead prayed with her and made sure she made it safely onto the bus.

"God has your back, Neveah. Don't worry. Everything is going to work out and you'll get to see your mother," he'd said.

Neveah entered the facility, not knowing exactly what the procedure was for visitation, but hoping after all of this planning, she would actually get to visit with her mother. She stepped to the counter and waited until the attendant was done with another person. Soon, she turned her attention to Neveah.

"May I help you?" she asked Neveah, not looking at her as she straightened items on the counter.

"Yes, um, I'm here to visit my mother."

"Do you have her prisoner number?"

"No, ma'am. I don't. Her name is Wyleena Richardson."

The woman went to a computer and pushed some buttons. Finally, she looked at Neveah for the first time and asked, "Do you have your ID?"

"Yes, ma'am." Neveah gave the woman her ID and she returned her attention to the computer screen and punched more buttons.

"Sign in here. Take this key and lock all of your belongings in a locker." The woman sat a key on the counter. "When you're done there, come back here and someone will escort you in. Be sure to hold onto that key. Let me see your hand."

Neveah held her hand out as the woman marked it with an invisible pen.

Neveah did as she was asked and went behind the big heavy door shortly thereafter. The sound of the metal door closing startled her. After being searched, she was led into a room where she sat to wait for her mother.

Neveah heard the feet shuffling before the door opened. Wyleena appeared with a guard escorting her. She wore an orange jumpsuit with a number marked on the pocket. Once her eyes landed on her daughter's, they never released them. She sat in front of Neveah, maintaining eye contact the entire time. Tears welled up, flooding her eyes until they leaked over the rims of her eyes and down her cheeks.

"I knew you would come looking for me," Wyleena said, a smile sneaking onto her lips.

"Is that why I was already on your visitor list?"

"Yes. How have you been?"

"It's been tough, Mama. Real tough. Are you okay? I've been worried about you."

"I'm okay, now that I can lay my eyes on you. But there's no need to lie, jail is no vacation spot but I'm going to be all right. Tell me what's been going on with you."

"I ended up in foster care. I had a good foster mother. I stayed there until one of the other foster children started molesting me."

Wyleena shook her head.

"She made him leave but he came back after he got hurt in a car accident. I didn't feel safe with him there so I left."

"Where did you go then?"

"I had my own apartment and when that didn't work out, I lived in a shelter for a while and then ended up with The Family of Saints."

"What's the Family of Saints?"

"It's a group that lives way out in the country in Ohio. They became my family since I was alone. It's led by a couple. She's really the leader and he's her assistant."

"Do they control your life?"

"There's a lot you can't do like have a Bible. Akadeus is god there and we kinda have to follow him and Nasia's direction or you're punished."

"Baby, I don't like the sound of this Family of Saints you're talking about. This Akadeus guy says he's God? That's a big red flag, honey. There's God with a big g and god with a small g. This Akadeus man is god with a small g. He's not the real God."

"You should see him. His eyes change colors, showing his emotion and he knows things that no one has told him."

"God is not in all of this hocus-pocus stuff. That's god with a small g." Wyleena got quiet for a few beats. "Wait a minute. Akadeus' eyes change colors?"

"Yes, it's the weirdest thing. I've never seen anyone's eyes do that."

"Hmm. There was a time I knew a man whose eyes did that. I was deeply in love with him. His name was Aaron. Ask Akadeus if his real name is Aaron."

"Who is Aaron, Mama?"

"Just ask him. There's no need to get into that right now if it's not him."

"Oookay. I met a man there named Art. He's my husband-mate."

"Husband-mate?"

"He takes care of me, he protects me, and he makes sure I have whatever I need. He said he's sent by God. He's been teaching me about Him."

"That's wonderful."

"He's the one who snuck to find out where you were and even put together the plan to get me out of the compound and here to you. He went out of his way and took a chance to do all of that."

"Does Art make you happy?"

"He's a good guy, but I don't know if I have time for a man."

"This man loves you. I can tell by what you've said about him. He even risked his own safety for you. That kind of love is difficult to find. Take a good long look at it and give it a chance. He could be the one God with the big g has for you."

Neveah thought about what Wyleena was saying about Art. She loved how she felt with him and she was pretty sure he cared about her beyond being her husband-mate. However, she really did want to focus on her life without having to see to a man's needs too.

"Is it Otis'?"

"What?"

Wyleena nodded toward Neveah's protruding belly. "The baby. Is it Otis'?"

Neveah dropped her head and whispered, "Yes, ma'am."

"Lift your head, Neveah. You have nothing to be ashamed of. The shame is mine. I should've been paying closer attention. I never would've thought Otis would do that to you. I've learned my lesson. No more men around you. Otis was the last."

"Mama, you don't have to protect me anymore. You deserve love, too. Don't let what happened keep you from having that if you want it."

"You see where I am and there's no men in here except these guards. Once I get out of here, I'm going to focus on you and my grandbaby." Neveah gave her the side-eye. "If a man comes along, I'll consider him. But you need to follow your own advice, too."

After Neveah left the prison, she thought about her mother's words regarding Art. He did seem to care about her but she wasn't sure if it was because it was part of his husband-mate assignment. He was certainly helpful to her and watched out for her.

Neveah also wasn't sure about her own feelings where Art was concerned. He was a wonderful guy and she had to admit she did feel an attraction to him. He was handsome with his curly brown hair and clean-cut appearance. He handled her thoughts and problems with a gentleness she'd never experienced from a man in her young life.

But Neveah had a lot on her plate. Leaving the Family of Saints, the birth of her baby, where she would live, and how she would survive were all on her mind and heart. These things wouldn't allow space for a man, no matter how wonderful he was.

CHAPTER 39

Neveah barged into the Pooles' abode with guards following behind her.

"I need to see Chief Saint Potentate Akadeus!"

Nasia appeared. "Um, I don't know what's wrong with you, but you don't get to just roll up in here like this."

Akadeus appeared shortly after Nasia. "What's going on?"

"I just saw my mother and she said something very interesting." Akadeus' eyes changed colors.

"Do you know a woman named Wyleena?"

Akadeus dropped his head.

Nasia asked, "Well, do you? What is this about?"

"Since you won't answer that question, I'll ask the one she told me to ask. Is your name Aaron?"

After a long pause, Akadeus said, "Yes, my name is Aaron and I do know Wyleena. I know who you are, too. Recognized you almost immediately."

"Recognized her? You know her? What's going on?" Nasia asked, with her gaze bouncing from Neveah to Akadeus.

"Neveah is my daughter."

Neveah's mouth dropped open. "You're my father?"

"Yes, I am."

"I can't even believe that."

"Why didn't you tell me you had a child?" Nasia asked, slapping Akadeus' arm.

"I didn't tell you because I was embarrassed. I've never been a father to Neveah."

"What kind of man fathers a child but doesn't participate in their upbringing?"

"The kind of man who had a bad enough drug problem that he was afraid he would mess his child up because of it."

"I didn't know you had a drug problem."

"None of that stuff matters at this point. I've been clean for a number of years and no longer even have the urge to use anymore."

"It matters that you misrepresented yourself to me."

"I'm the guy you married regardless of my lack of parenting and the drug problem I had in the past." Akadeus refocused on Neveah. He went to her and reached for her hands. She allowed him to hold them as he spoke to her. "I always kept up with you, because I always loved and cared about you. I just didn't want to be a problem in your life because of my issues. I hope you'll forgive my absence and will give us a chance to develop a relationship."

"This is so overwhelming. I don't know how to respond," Neveah said as she shook her head in disbelief.

"I'm sure you have a lot of questions and I'm here to answer them all."

CHAPTER 40

Neveah and Art entered her apartment and immediately fell onto her couch. The happenings of the previous hour had been both eye-opening and shocking. No one said a word as they each processed what they discovered.

"Wow, that was interesting, wasn't it?" Art asked.

"I can't believe Akadeus is my father. I don't even know how to feel about that."

"I'm sure. I would probably feel the same way."

"I spent most of my life thinking he was dead and now to see him face-to-face is a huge surprise."

"You want something to drink?" Neveah asked, opening her refrigerator.

"Yes, I'll take some bottled water if you have it."

Neveah returned with two bottles of water, handed a bottle to Art and took a swig from the one she'd opened for herself.

"Now that you've found him, do you think you'll stick around here and get to know him?"

"I haven't even thought that far ahead, but I guess I should consider it."

"I think you should stay and spend some time with him, get to know him. Not just for yourself, but for your child, too. Grandparents are the best."

"That's all true but I might want to go back to Michigan at some point."

"What would that mean for us?" Art scooted to the edge of his seat and focused his attention directly on Neveah.

"You can come to Michigan with me."

"I would like nothing more, but I need to stay here to complete my assignment."

"I thought I was your assignment."

Art thought a beat. "You're right."

"And you've completed that assignment, right?"

"I have."

"So why do you have to stay?"

"Leaving is a little more complicated than it appears."

"What's complicated about it?"

"Just suffice it to say it's not as simple as packing up and walking out."

***

Later that night as Art laid on his bed, he thought about the possibility of leaving The Family of Saints. The idea had never crossed his mind before. He had simply resigned himself to being there for the foreseeable future. Neveah had unexpectedly planted a seed of thought in Art's mind.

He'd been close to Akadeus and Nasia for many years, which ultimately led to his service to The Family of Saints. Truthfully, his time there hadn't been bad and he'd come to realize his purpose for being there was much bigger than what it initially appeared to be. However, he'd never thought about whether this was what he wanted to do for the rest of his life. Now that he believed his higher purpose was achieved, would he continue to stay? Was he willing to risk his relationship with Neveah?

As the sun rose, he realized he hadn't slept but wrestled all night with the weight of the predicament. However, he had made a decision. One he would follow through on regardless of what Neveah decided to do though he made it with her in mind. Something he wouldn't have even considered even twelve hours ago. Art was going to leave The Family of Saints. But, in true Art form, he couldn't just be concerned about himself, he also considered his husband-mate comrades. If there was a possibility he could help just one of them gain their freedom, it would be worth a try.

CHAPTER 41

Art went around and spoke to all of the husband-mates, explaining his plan to leave the Family of Saints. As he'd thought about the possibilities for his life that would come from being free from the Family of Saints, he became energized and hoped he could convince all of the others this was the right thing to do. It would work best if the majority of the husband-mates agreed and cooperated.

"Look guys, I know you're scared, but I think it's time we stood up to Nasia and reclaim our lives." Art looked each man in the eyes as he challenged them to consider his ideas.

"But what will we do then? Most of us have been doing this for several years."

"I believe God will create other options for us. Have a little faith," Art explained.

"I guess I would like to go home and see if my girlfriend will take me back. She wasn't exactly excited about me coming here," one husband-mate said.

Another spoke up and said, "I could probably go back to school."

"There's something you all aren't thinking about," said Joseph, the eldest of the husband-mates. "We could all go to jail."

"We're already in jail. So, what would be the difference?"

"At least here I have a little freedom. Behind bars, things would be a lot different," Joseph reasoned.

"Think about it, how long have we been doing this? Where does it end? Nasia might not ever let us go voluntarily." Art presented an alternative perspective.

The men were silent, apparently mulling over the words Art spoke to them.

After a couple of minutes, he stuck his hand out. "Who's in?"

One by one, all of the men laid their hand across the hand below it as a sign of agreement until everyone committed to the effort. All that was left to do was carry out their plan, believe God was with them and see what happened.

***

Every husband-mate, whether assigned at the time or not, marched to the clearing and began shouting. One of the Pooles' guards was summoned then asked to contact the leaders and have them come down for a meeting.

When the Pooles arrived and were seated, they asked for the husband-mates to share their concerns.

"We're tired of being husband-mates. We want our freedom."

"Is that right?" Nasia asked.

"Yes, it is."

The crowd yelled their agreement behind Art's statement.

Nasia looked at Akadeus as his eyes changed color.

"What do you think?"

"I think you need to make a decision since you're the leader."

Nasia thought momentarily before speaking, "You all can't leave. You owe me," she said, jabbing her finger toward the men. We all committed the crime but I did all the time while y'all had fun spending that money." Nasia scanned the crowd before pointing at one of the men. "Josh, you don't think I know about that new house you and your wife built?" She pointed at another man and said, "Mason, I know your boys went to that expensive private school, too. I know what y'all did even though I was locked up."

"We've been serving the Family of Saints for several years. We're quite sure we've more than paid you back. Will we be paying you back for the rest of our lives?"

"Oh, is that what this little protest is about? You've paid me back when I say you've paid me back"

"I owe you. Not them. Let them go," Akadeus said.

"Un-huh, I covered for all of you so all of y'all owe me. I hold all of the cards. Just as a woman should."

"Baby, these men are right. You can't hold them hostage forever because I messed up. We need to work this out between the two of us and let them get on with their lives."

"You all can leave whenever you like. But I'll be forced to contact the authorities and report your involvement in what we were doing, though."

"I figured you would say that, Nasia," Art said. "But, do you realize you'll be sending your own husband to jail, too?"

"I know we were wrong running that scheme and I shouldn't have let you take the fall for all of us," Akadeus said, waving his hand across the crowd. "I'm in this because you said that was the only way I could be with you. Can we be together without the Family of Saints? Can you let this whole thing go and focus on us?"

"I don't know but I'll think about it." Nasia turned her attention to the husband-mates. "As for all of you, I was serious when I said you could leave whenever you want. But I promise I will report each of you to the police. So, think hard before you make your decision."

***

"So, what do we do now?" One of the husband-mates asked.

"I should've known Nasia wasn't just going to let us go without a fight," another lamented.

Art listened carefully to the complaints of his fellow husband-mates. They were all clearly dejected and frustrated and he completely understood their feelings. However, Art's perspective had become broader since he'd met Neveah. He believed their relationship was destined to be something greater than what it could be within The Family of Saints and he intended to pursue it. Staying was no longer an option for him, regardless of what the consequences might be.

"I'm leaving, guys. I'm not doing this any longer."

"But, Nasia will probably have you prosecuted."

"I don't know if she'll really do that, because Akadeus would end up in jail, too."

"You heard her. Akadeus is in the same boat as the rest of us, except he gets to sit on the chair next to Nasia. Other than that, I don't think she cares any more about him than she does us, to tell the truth."

Art considered this argument and it was valid. It was true that Nasia seemed willing to turn Akadeus in to the authorities, along with any of the husband-mates that left. But Art had to decide whether his freedom from The Family of Saints was more important to him.

"I'm still leaving. I'd rather be temporarily imprisoned if it means I can be permanently free afterward. If I stay here, I might be a husband-mate for the rest of my life and I refuse to do that. I'm not giving Nasia any more power to make decisions about my life."

"I bet Neveah is the reason you're so anxious to get out of here."

A huge grin slowly developed on Art's face. "I won't deny that, but even if I didn't know her, I would still want to end this arrangement no matter the cost."

"Well, God bless you, Art. I hope everything works out for you."

"So, who else is leaving? Anyone?"

The group, including Art, looked at one another, waiting for someone to speak up. Finally, a hand went up, then another, then another until every man present had indicated they were in agreement to leave The Family of Saints.

"Okay, guys. We just have to set a date and make our move."

CHAPTER 42

The day finally came when the husband-mates would defect. They had all packed whatever belongings they had. They had agreed to march out at the same time directly after saying goodbye to the women they were assigned to at the time.

There was a knock on Neveah's door. She knew it was Art wanting to say "goodbye" so she lingered a while before answering. She didn't want him to leave since neither knew exactly where they were going to land.

"Neveah, I know you're in there. Please open the door," Art pleaded.

Neveah meandered toward the door, not wanting to face Art for what could be the last time. She opened the door and saw him standing there with a duffle bag hanging from his shoulder. When she looked in his eyes, she saw the same sadness she believed was present in hers.

Art slowly slipped the bag off of his shoulder and sat it on the floor. He approached Neveah, took her hands in his, and gazed in her eyes. He slowly moved closer and planted a soft kiss on her lips.

Neveah closed her eyes as she savored the tenderness of his kiss. How could she let this man leave her? How could she leave their relationship to chance, hoping they would be able to find each other once Neveah left the compound.

"I can't believe you're leaving without me," Neveah whispered.

"I have to go with the rest of the guys after I talked them into leaving," Art responded. "This is only temporary. We'll find each other once you leave here."

"How do you know? Are you willing to take that chance?"

"I don't want to leave you, but this is the way things worked out. You need to stay so you can get to know your father and I need to leave. I don't see any other way."

Neveah released Art's hands. She turned her back to him to hide the threat of tears. She didn't want him to feel guilty about doing what he had to do. After all, she was doing what was best for her as well. Or was she? She returned her gaze to Art.

"Excuse me a minute," she said, moving toward her bedroom.

"Neveah, don't be mad at me. You know I love you."

Neveah stopped walking but didn't face Art.

"You love me?" Neveah asked.

"You know I do," Art responded.

Neveah walked away from Art into her bedroom. When she returned to the living room, she noticed Art was heading toward the door with his duffle bag.

"Hey," she said. "Are you leaving without me?"

Art exhaled loudly and turned toward the woman he'd unexpectedly fallen in love with. "We've already been through this…"

"I'm going with you. Let's go."

Art smiled and asked, "Are you sure? What about Akadeus?"

"If I'm going to take a chance on not seeing someone, it's going to be my father since he's never been in my life to begin with."

"Let's go before you come to your senses," Art said, taking the bags from Neveah's hands.

The two skipped out of the room as the other husband-mates were leaving the buildings. Neveah looked up and saw Niecy gawking at the parade leaving. She went toward her and hugged her tightly.

"Thanks for everything, Niecy. I hope you find your way."

Niecy fought back tears as she waved goodbye to her friend.

The husband-mates were already boarding the bus when Neveah and Art exited the building.

Akadeus and Nasia were in the area as well. As Nasia threatened the men with prosecution, Akadeus focused on Neveah and Art. He caught up with his daughter and tapped her on the shoulder.

"What's going on, Neveah? Where are you going?" Akadeus asked her.

"All of the husband-mates are leaving," Neveah said, not wanting to look her father in the eyes for fear he might convince her to change her mind.

"I know that, but where are you going?"

"I decided to go with Art."

"You were just going to leave without telling me?"

"I couldn't tell you the husband-mates were leaving because I promised I wouldn't say anything. I decided I was leaving with Art about ten minutes ago."

"Please stay. I don't want to lose touch with you now that we have a chance at a real relationship."

"I've already made my decision and I'm going with Art. I hope you understand."

Akadeus' shoulders slumped and his countenance changed. Neveah's heart broke because of her father's apparent sadness about her leaving. She never thought she would have the opportunity to meet her father or get to know him and yet, though she had met him, she was leaving him to be with the man she loved.

With Nasia still fussing in the background, Akadeus told Neveah, "I'm coming too. I can't let you walk out of my life. Give me a minute."

Neveah was surprised and pleased that both of the new men in her life would be on this new journey with her.

Without saying goodbye to his wife, Akadeus climbed aboard the bus along with the other guys. As the driver started the bus, Nasia rushed the door and demanded the driver open it. Her eyes met Akadeus'.

She yelled over the sound of the bus and the ruckus of the crowd, "I thought you were staying with me, Akadeus."

"My daughter is leaving and I want to have a chance to develop a relationship with her."

"But I need you. You can't leave."

Akadeus exited the bus and hugged his wife close and said, "I was thinking we can help the people that are left to find someplace else to live. Then, we can shut this compound down and get a fresh start somewhere close to my daughter. We can all go to my sister Monique's house until we get back on our feet. Please, Nasia. I'm begging you. I really want to be with you."

Nasia pushed herself away from her husband and pounded her fist into his chest. "You must be out of your mind. I'm not going to your sister's house. I didn't even know you had one."

Akadeus backed away from Nasia slowly. "Then I guess this is it for now. You made your choice, now I have to make mine." He hugged her, kissing her gently on her forehead. "I'll get in contact with you when I get settled. Maybe you will have changed your mind by then. I love you, Nasia, but I have to go."

"You don't love me. If you did, you wouldn't be leaving right now. You can have your little daughter. When she breaks your heart, you'll be running back to me but I won't take you back, Akadeus. I'm telling you, I won't."

He turned and walked away from her. She grabbed his clothing, trying to keep him from leaving. He removed her hands from his garments, got on the bus, and situated himself in his seat. The driver put the bus in gear and pulled off.

"Where are you going with my bus?" Nasia yelled, trotting beside the vehicle as it moved toward the road. "You'd better leave my bus here. This is my bus," she yelled.

The bus kept moving and Nasia finally gave up her pursuit. Neveah watched as Nasia slumped to the ground. She felt terrible for Nasia and Akadeus. She wished they'd had the time to discuss this decision and come to a conclusion they both could deal with. However, time hadn't allowed that.

Neveah viewed her father and saw his sadness.

"Akadeus," she spoke to get his attention. "Are you sure you want to leave?"

Akadeus swiped at the tears gathering on his face. "No, but I've made my decision and I'm sticking with it."

"But you and Nasia love each other and I think you'll be miserable without each other."

"I'm not going back. If we're going to be together, it's not going to be in that compound and she's not ready to let it go yet."

Neveah sat back in her seat. She'd tried her best to help her father salvage his marriage and it hadn't worked. Ultimately, it was a decision Akadeus and Nasia had to make for themselves. Neveah didn't have enough influence to make that happen.

CHAPTER 43

The bus was silent as it sped along the highway. They had been on the road for over an hour since they left The Family of Saints compound. Neveah noticed just about everyone on the vehicle was asleep except Akadeus, who stared out of the window. His downturned lips and teary eyes revealed the deep sadness that existed. Neveah knewhe was heartbroken and she was concerned about him. She reached over and squeezed his shoulder in an attempt to comfort him the best way she could.

"Maybe you should call and talk to Nasia. You did just jump on the bus and leave without really talking to her."

Neveah wasn't sure if Akadeus heard her, based on his lack of a response. She sat back in her seat, allowing her father time with his own thoughts. He got up and went to the back of the bus with his cell phone. Neveah hoped he was going to call Nasia. Otherwise, she believed he was going to be unhappy.

She looked at Art whose head was leaning against the window, snoring and drooling on the bench across the aisle from her. She smiled as she thought about the prospects of their relationship outside of The Family of Saints. Her baby kicked and stretched out within her.

"You like Art too don't you, little one?"

A pain ripped through her abdomen then disappeared. It appeared again a few moments later and left her again. The pain became so intense she bent over in pain.

"Art! Wake up!"

Art sprung up from the bench and stared into space briefly before his eyes closed once again.

"I'm in labor."

Art's eyes sprung open and he hurried to her side.

"Did you say you're in labor?"

"I've never had a baby before, but I think so."

After completing her sentence, she realized a trickle of water flowed into the seat eventually spilling onto the floor.

"I think you might be right."

Art went to the front of the bus to speak to the driver and ask him to point the vehicle in the direction of the nearest hospital.

"We'll have to watch the signs on the side of the highway and hopefully we'll find one soon," the bus driver responded, glancing back at Art.

Akadeus noticed the flurry of activity and returned to his daughter's side. "Is everything okay?"

Neveah's face scrunched from the pain as tears flowed down her face. "I think I'm getting ready to have my baby."

Akadeus shot up and frantically looked around the bus for help. "Is Dr. Will on the bus?"

"I'm here. What do you need?" Dr. Will asked, walking up the aisle.

"My daughter appears to be in labor. Do you know how to deliver a baby?"

"I've delivered a few, but we should really try to find a hospital. How far apart are her contractions?"

"I don't know. We'll have to time them and find out."

"If this is her first child, we could be waiting for hours."

"Let's just hope we get to a hospital before we have to deliver the baby here."

Dr. Will sat in front of Neveah, timing her contractions and encouraging her to breathe through each one.

"She's in labor and her contractions are about five minutes apart," Dr. Will said, staring at his watch. He looked up at a concerned Art. "We might have to deliver this baby right on the bus if we don't find a hospital soon."

Akadeus yelled to the driver, "Did you find a hospital?"

The driver responded, "Not yet."

Neveah let out a moan, indicating the pain was getting worse.

Dr. Will whispered to Akadeus, "I need to examine her."

"Go ahead. Examine her."

"You don't understand. I have to check to see how much she's dilated."

"What are you saying?"

"Dilation expands the opening the baby comes through," Dr. Will said, with a pointed look.

"Oh, this is my daughter! There will be no exam on this bus."

"This baby doesn't care about any of that. Your daughter is about to become a mother regardless."

"You are not looking at her down there!"

Neveah let out a growl.

The driver crossed two lanes of traffic and directed the bus to the side of the road. Murmuring broke out as everyone wondered why the bus was pulling over.

"Why are you pulling over?" Akadeus asked the driver. "We need to keep things moving so we can get my daughter to a hospital."

"It's the police. I don't know why they're stopping us."

Akadeus looked out of the window and saw three police cars escorting them to the side of the road.

"Nasia must've called them."

Akadeus wondered what was going to happen when the police boarded the bus as they would surely do. He'd just tried calling Nasia and she didn't answer. Did she follow through on her promise to call the police on them? What did she tell them? Was this about the bus or did she tell them about the crime they'd all participated in? Would everyone go to jail? Akadeus and the people on this bus would find out in a few moments, because the officers were climbing on.

"Hi Officer, what can we do for you?" the driver asked.

"Do you know why we pulled you over?"

"No, sir. I don't."

"You have a broken taillight and your vehicle registration is expired."

Akadeus released the breath he was holding.

Neveah screamed as another contraction hit.

The officer put his hand on his revolver and requested everyone to take a seat as he moved toward Neveah.

"Ma'am, are you okay?"

"I'm in labor."

"Officer, can you help us get my daughter to a hospital?"

The officer gestured for Akadeus to step away. He scrutinized her then looked at the floor around her seat where the amniotic fluid had gathered.

"Ma'am, we'll get to the hospital right away." He walked to the exit and told the driver, "We'll escort you there so we don't have to move her."

Moments later, the caravan began moving. The rickety bus raced over the twists and turns of the winding road causing Neveah to be tossed about a little.

"I'm scared," Neveah whispered to Art who was comforting her from his seat behind her.

"Don't be. Remember, God loves you and He's going to take good care of you and the baby."

Neveah remembered those words that had been spoken to her many times over the course of the past several years. When Otis said those words, it was to manipulate her to think what he was doing to her was a reflection of God's love. Her experience at the church when she'd seen the posters led her to believe God only loved those who fit the criteria of the people in that church. Now, after spending time with Art, she knew what God's love really felt like. She knew what Art had been showing her was authentic. It was God's love and there were no strings attached.

Neveah smiled and slowly nodded her head, "Yeah, God does love me, doesn't He?"

Art smiled and dotted Neveah's forehead with kisses. "I'm so glad you know that now."

The caravan pulled into the parking lot of a small hospital a few miles off of the freeway. Hospital staff took Neveah off the bus and disappeared inside the hospital with her. She was still scared but felt slightly better, because she was in the hands of people who knew exactly what to do and could get her through the process.

After answering what seemed like a hundred questions, getting changed into a gown and being examined, it was discovered Neveah was dilated to six centimeters. She would soon meet the baby that had been living inside of her throughout her ordeal. She wondered if the baby was a boy or a girl. She hoped the baby looked like her and not Otis. It would be difficult to look into her baby's face and see her abuser. Yet, she knew it was a possibility and if it were the case, she was sure she would love her baby anyway.

Later, Neveah was prepped for delivery. She requested Art come into the birthing room with her. It took him so long to appear she thought perhaps he refused to come.

Neveah looked up as Art came into the room covered from head to toe in protective garb to help maintain a certain level of sterility in the room. Though his mouth and nose were covered, Neveah could tell he was smiling by looking in his eyes.

"You really want me to be with you when your baby is born?"

"I need you. Are you okay with that?"

"Right now I am, but I might end up on the floor."

They each chuckled.

"I've never done this either, so we'll learn together."

The team came into the room and prepared to deliver Neveah's baby. Though she had been afraid earlier, she was now excited to meet this little one who had been kicking, elbowing, and stretching out inside of her. How would she raise this person? What would she do about a job in order to take care of him or her? Who would babysit while she worked? All of these questions ran through Neveah's mind as the doctor got into position to usher her baby into the world.

CHAPTER 44

Art and Akadeus looked on adoringly as Neveah cuddled her new baby girl. Chubby cheeks, a headful of curly jet-black hair and skin the color of light brown sugar peeked out from the pink swaddling. Neveah had counted fingers and toes to ensure the baby had everything she was supposed to have.

"She's beautiful," Akadeus said as a proud grandfather.

"What are you going to name her?" Art asked, peeking at the bundle from the opposite side of the bed.

"I haven't decided yet, but I think it has to begin with an 'A'." Neveah smiled as the two new men in her life realized the baby would be named in their honor. "I'm so glad I have the two of you in my life. I don't know where I'd be if it wasn't for you guys."

"You would've been just fine. After all you've been through you've proven you're a survivor," Art responded, caressing Neveah's face.

Akadeus remained quiet as he watched the exchange between Neveah and Art.

"I wish my mother was here. She would've loved to be a part of this."

"We'll see what we can do about that a little later," Art stated.

Neveah noticed Akadeus' facial expression and could only imagine he was thinking about Nasia. There wasn't much Neveah could do about Nasia and Akadeus' relationship issues, but she could try to cheer him up in some small way.

"Do you want to hold her, Granddad?"

"I would love to."

Art transferred the newborn from Neveah's arms into Akadeus', who sat in the recliner next to the bed. He rocked the baby, who rewarded him with a smile. The baby girl had captured his heart already.

"Art and I need to find a store to purchase some things you'll need right away for the baby. I know they won't let you leave the hospital without a car seat. We'll also have to get clothing, diapers, socks, blankets, a cradle, bottles and formula and I'm sure there's some other items you'll need."

"I appreciate you guys. I haven't even thought about that stuff. I can't pay you for all of this right now, but once I get a job and get everything together, I will."

Akadeus stood and placed the baby in her mother's arms. "I'm not accepting any money from you. I know I haven't acted like it, but I am your father. Let me be your father and her grandfather. I owe the two of you that much. I want to be there for both of you."

"I know we have a lot of catching up to do, but I'm an adult and my daughter is my responsibility. You can just be a grandparent."

"This is being a grandparent. All I want you to do is relax and enjoy this beautiful baby girl. When we get to Monique's house, you need to take it easy for a while so you can recover. Don't argue with me about this. This is just how it's going to be."

Akadeus leaned over and kissed Neveah on the forehead. "I love you, Neveah and grandbaby, whose name starts with 'A'. Don't worry. I'm going to take good care of you."

***

Two days later, the Uber pulled up to Monique's house. Neveah nervously unfastened the infant carrier her daughter, Artrice, was snoozing in. Before she could open the door, Art was there opening it and taking the child from her.

"I'll take her. You need to take it easy."

Akadeus removed the car seat's base and exited the car. He went to the trunk and removed the bags of baby things.

Neveah stood back and let Akadeus go ahead of her so she could gauge Monique's reaction to her, the baby, and Art coming to stay in her home.

The door flung open and Monique rushed out. Neveah noticed Monique had cut her hair in a cute short style and had lost some weight, but appeared ecstatic to see Akadeus. The siblings embraced then held a quiet conversation with each other.

"What are you doing here?"

"It's a long story but I need a place to stay. We need some place to stay," Akadeus said, gesturing toward the group. "And before you even ask, I'm clean."

When the two separated, Monique peeked around her brother at Art, Neveah, and finally Artrice. Her scrunched up face revealed her true feelings about the group who accompanied Akadeus.

"Neveah? Is that you?"

"Yes, Auntie Monique, it is," Neveah said, stepping forward.

"Whose baby is this?"

"She's mine," Neveah whispered, wondering what her aunt's response would be.

Monique shook her head, releasing a sigh.

"Come on in. There's no need to talk about all of this out here."

Everyone went inside and settled into Monique's family room.

"Hey, Monique, have you seen my…" A man appeared with a towel wrapped around his waist. Judging by the bare feet and glistening bare chest, he had just gotten out of the shower. "I didn't know you were expecting guests."

"They surprised me, too. This is my brother Aaron, my niece Neveah and," Monique gestured to Art, "I'm sorry. I didn't catch your name."

"I'm Art, ma'am," Art said, extending his hand to shake the man's hand.

"Well, hello everyone. I'm Everette," the man said, displaying the whitest teeth Neveah had ever seen.

"Don't be looking at my man like that, Neveah. See, that's why I wouldn't let you stay here when you called me and told me you needed someplace to go. Everette, go on back there in the bedroom so you won't be tempting my niece."

Everette shook his head, laughed and left the room.

"What was that all about and why wouldn't you let Neveah stay with you?"

"Oh, she didn't tell you about that?" a sarcastic Monique snarled at Neveah, leaving her feeling as though he had done something to be ashamed of.

"What's there to tell that would make you leave her in the streets? You do know she didn't have any place to go, right?" Akadeus frowned and leaned forward to hear what his sister's reasoning was.

"She told me her stepfather was raping her, but I know she really seduced him. I don't know if she was trying to come between him and her mother or what. I couldn't have that here in my home with Everette. We have a good thing going and I don't want her to mess it up."

"Auntie Monique, I don't know why you don't believe me, but I'm telling the truth about Otis. I was excited when Mama met him and they got together because that meant I finally had a father. Why would I want to break them up? I loved Otis...at first, anyway." Akadeus appeared distressed. "But he hadn't been living with us very long when he started touching me and making me touch him. I was too young to know what was happening was wrong, though it didn't feel right. It progressed until he was having sex with me most nights because Mama was at work. That little girl over there is Otis' child."

Akadeus' fists clenched and unclenched several times as his face turned red and his jaw tightened. "Where do I find this Otis? I need to deal with him man-to-man."

"She didn't tell you that either? Otis is dead. Neveah convinced Wyleena that Otis was messing with her and Wyleena killed him. She's serving time right now because of this girl's lies."

"Monique, I'm just about tired of you talking about Neveah like she was responsible for all of this. She was a child and he was an adult." Akadeus' eyes turned to red as he defended his daughter.

"But you didn't know Otis. He wasn't the type of man she's making him out to be. He would never get involved with her unless she forced herself on him. That's the Otis I knew."

"Neveah is telling you this man sexually abused her, even to the point her mother killed him, yet you're defending him and I'm trying to understand why. Now, I'm going to ask you something and I don't want you to be offended. Were you involved with Otis?"

"Why would you think that?"

"Because I know you, Monique, and you didn't deny being involved with him. Now what's going on?"

Monique took and released a deep breath, causing her shoulders to rise and fall. "Otis and I met each other first. He and I had a friends-with-benefits relationship and I was good with that for a while. I eventually fell in love with Otis, though I never told him. I understood our arrangement and didn't think he would continue seeing me if I told him I loved him. I introduced him to Wyleena at one of my birthday parties, not knowing they would hit it off and get married. Otis and I continued our relationship for a while, then one day he decided to end it, though I was willing to stay in my place. I would've done anything, including being the side-chick, just to be near him, hear him laugh and feel his touch. I was heartbroken and couldn't figure out why he would feel that way. But now I know why. It's because your little girl seduced him and he didn't need me like that anymore."

"You don't even believe that. You're just trying to blame Otis' decision on somebody else because you can't accept the fact he made the decision himself. He used you and he didn't want you anymore because he got married, not because of Neveah."

"You can't accept Neveah is promiscuous."

"But, I'm not promiscuous. Otis is the only man I've ever been with."

"I don't know who you think you're fooling, Neveah. I know he's the father." Monique jabbed her finger in Art's direction.

"He's not. I was already pregnant when I met Art and besides, Art and I have never been intimate."

"Then who's the father?"

"I told you. It's Otis." Neveah's voice carried an edge that bordered on disrespect, but she was done carrying the shame caused by what Otis did to her. She realized her mother was right. It didn't belong to her. It belonged to Otis. "And before you say I wanted it, I did not. I was forced. I'm sorry my experience challenges your impression of Otis. This is the last time I'm going to explain this to you, Auntie Monique. You either believe me or you don't."

Neveah rose from her seat and took Artrice out of her carrier. "Is there someplace I can feed and change my baby?"

"Go through there, go to your right, it's the first room on the left," Monique reluctantly directed her.

The room was silent as everyone watched Neveah leave the room in a huff.

As Neveah dealt with her baby, she heard Akadeus and Monique arguing with each other. Neveah surely didn't want to cause a feud between them but she knew Akadeus well enough to know he would defend her. Art had been silent since they arrived, but she heard him trying to calm the situation. She smiled, realizing this was his normal demeanor. He was a soothing force in every situation and she needed that in her life, given everything she had experienced and everything that lie ahead.

She completed her task and took a good look at her little bundle. The baby was precious and Neveah felt honored to be her mother. She couldn't wait to get settled so she could provide a stable environment for her daughter to grow up in. There would be no chaos and if there was, she would be sure her child was completely unaware of it. She would develop a close and loving relationship with her just as Wyleena and done with her. Though Neveah didn't blame her mother for what happened to her, she would be much more careful with her own daughter to insure her safety at all costs. She would also make sure her child knew she was loved. Not just by her mother, but also by God. That revelation had made a positive difference in Neveah's life and she believed her daughter would benefit from it as well.

Neveah stepped out of her safe haven back into the family room where Monique, Akadeus, and Art sat. A moment later, Everette entered the room as well, carrying a duffle bag over his shoulder and another bag in his hand, causing Monique to be obviously startled and concerned.

"Wh..wh… Where are you going?" Monique stuttered.

"I'm going back to my place while your family is here. I overheard what you all were talking about and I don't want to be a concern for you. I would never do anything to harm anyone but I don't want you to have to wonder about that. They need you and I think you should be there for them."

"Are you breaking up with me because of them? I didn't even know they were coming!"

"No, that's not what this is, though after hearing how you feel about your niece, I'm wondering who you really are. You're welcome to come visit me and I don't mind coming by here from time to time, but I think it's important for you all to focus on each other right now. I'll call you in the morning."

With that, Everette left Monique's house with her following him, begging him not to go. But, Everette got in his car and left.

Neveah braced herself for what she thought would be an angry tirade from Auntie Monique, blaming her for her boyfriend leaving. She hugged her baby close and waited to see what would happen. She had never seen this side of Auntie Monique and it surprised her. She almost came across as desperate and Neveah had always seen Monique as self-confident and secure.

The screen door closed and everyone's eyes settled on Monique. To Neveah's surprise, she was dejected and not angry. Neveah allowed herself to relax.

"Y'all can stay. Just give me a few minutes to get myself together, then I'll show you where everything is."

With that, Monique left the room and went to what Neveah figured was her bedroom and closed the door. Afterwards, Neveah heard her crying though she didn't understand why, since Everette was only giving them time and space to get to know one another. Perhaps Monique's tears had more to do with what she learned about Otis today. Neveah wasn't sure but would ask her aunt about it later when she felt the time was right.

CHAPTER 45

The first week of their stay at Monique's house had been filled with adjustments. Though Akadeus and Monique were both missing their significant others, Neveah was most concerned about Monique. Her mood hadn't lifted at all. Everette had come by for a visit once or twice but he went home each night despite Monique's begging.

Neveah had heard Akadeus talking to Nasia a number of times. From what she could hear, Akadeus was still trying to talk her into joining them. Though what she heard of their conversations seemed to be light, Neveah could also tell that Nasia was still angry at her husband for abandoning her. Akadeus remained patient and continued to declare his love for his wife.

Neveah was getting accustomed to being a mother. Getting up in the middle of the night to feed and cuddle with her baby was a huge adjustment that she wouldn't trade for anything in the world. The baby loved to snuggle and had a way of connecting with Neveah by looking directly into her eyes in a way that surprised Neveah and helped to grow their bond.

She and Art continued spending a lot of time together. He had even helped her with the baby such as feeding and bathing. Changing poopy diapers wasn't something he enjoyed, but he promised he would work on doing so.

The doorbell rang followed by pounding on the door.

"Who is it?" Monique asked through the door.

"Police."

Monique looked at Akadeus and Art who sighed and looked at each other. Akadeus went to the door and opened it. On the other side he found one officer and a few standing several feet away with their hands on their revolvers.

"Hi, Officer," Akadeus viewed the man's badge, "Reynolds. What can we do for you?"

"We're looking for Aaron aka Akadeus Poole and Art Gean."

"I'm Akadeus and that's Art," Akadeus said, pointing at Art who responded with a brief wave.

"We need you two to come down to the station to discuss a report we got from someone named Nasia Poole."

"For what?"

"We'll talk about that at the station."

"Alright, we'll come with you."

"We will?" Art asked. Akadeus shot him a look. "If we don't have to, I don't think we should voluntarily go. I mean, I'm just saying," Art said with a shrug.

"Come on, man. We know what this is about." Akadeus exited the house with Art reluctantly following.

"What's going on?" Neveah said with her voice cracking, following Art as far as the door.

"Don't worry guys. I'll call Everette. He's an attorney," Monique said as she left the door and went to call her boyfriend.

"Don't worry, honey. Everything will be okay," Art said, as Neveah crumbled to the floor.

Akadeus and Art left with the officers, who handcuffed them once they were outside and led them to a police car.

***

After the police drove away with Akadeus and Art, Neveah realized she and Monique were alone with each other for the first time since the trio arrived. The tension between them since they arrived was even more stifling that day. Neveah wasn't prepared to face it alone and sought a way to escape it at any cost.

"I need to check on the baby." Neveah shifted her weight from one foot to the other. "Excuse me," Neveah whispered as she headed to her bedroom.

"Can we talk for a minute?" Neveah halted her movement. "Please." Monique gestured toward the couch.

Neveah wasn't interested in hearing any more hurtful accusations, but decided to oblige her aunt since she was living in her house and felt it would be rude to ignore her.

Neveah didn't say a word as she walked past Monique and sat on the couch. Monique sat next to her niece but didn't speak. Finally, she wrapped Neveah in a hug, causing a dam of emotion to break somewhere on the inside of the young mother. Monique rocked her as she allowed her niece to empty her pain on to her shoulder.

Soon, Neveah's sobbing became a light whimper.

"Are you okay?" Monique continued comforting Neveah.

"I just feel like everyone that means anything to me keeps being taken away. It's not fair."

"You have me." Monique flashed a bright smile at Neveah.

Neveah pulled away from Monique and pondered her response. She had lost a significant amount of respect for her aunt. It was one thing to have a relationship with a man before he got married. It was another thing to continue on with him once he married your friend. Neveah was also flabbergasted that Monique would even think she would throw herself at Otis, of all people.

She looked Monique square in the eyes. "I do? See, I don't think so. Aside from at happened between you and Otis, you accused me of seducing him. How could you even think that? You have known me my whole life. You watched me grow up. What you told my father about me over the years caused him to be proud of me. Now all of a sudden, I'm like some whore or something who seduced my stepfather, causing him to leave you. What kind of person do you think I am? What kind of woman are you?"

"I'm a different person now than I was then and..."

"Oh yeah? When did the change happen because if my memory serves me correctly, it wasn't that long ago you left me homeless because of what happened back then. You really hurt my feelings."

"It all caught me at a crazy moment..."

"What kind of crazy moment did you have that would cause you to act the way you did toward me? Huh? I need to know because it makes absolutely no sense to me."

"I was in shock about Otis. I was still in love with him. There's no excuse for what I said and did to you. I was completely wrong and I apologize. Please forgive me."

Neveah recalled Art talking to her about the importance of forgiveness. Auntie Monique's actions had caused her a great deal of pain but, though it might take a while, Neveah knew what her response should be. "I don't know if our relationship will ever be the same, but I do forgive you."

"Thank you, honey. I really am sorry. I want to be there to help you and Artrice as much as I can."

"I'm going to need all the help I can get. But, right now, I'm worried about Akadeus and Art."

CHAPTER 46

Everette, Akadeus and Art rushed from the police station once the questioning ended without an arrest. The trio moved with purpose as they headed toward the exit.

"We appreciate you coming down here to help us." Akadeus patted Everette on the back. "I don't know what would have happened if you hadn't showed up."

"Just thinking about being locked up shook me up," Art said, shaking his head.

"I can't even imagine how Nasia felt doing the time she did," Akadeus uttered as his voice trailed off.

"I'm glad I could help you guys but this may not be over. They still might decide to go forward with charges later so you guys are going to need representation," Everette said, looking back at Akadeus and Art.

"I thought you were our lawyer," Art responded.

The men stood by Everette's vehicle, waiting for Everette to allow them entry.

"If I'm going to represent you guys, I need to know exactly what's going on here. If I get the feeling you're not being honest with me, I'll drop you with a quickness. You're going to have to answer every question I have about this situation. You okay with that?"

"We'll tell you everything you want to know. It's time we get this off our chests. You agree, Art?"

"Yes, I do. I'm tired of this being held over my head and I'm ready to deal with it and move on. Whatever you want to know, my man, I'll tell you."

Everette unlocked the car doors, effectively giving Akadeus and Art permission to enter.

Akadeus chuckled while getting into the car. "What would've happened if we hadn't agreed to your terms? Would you have left us here?"

"Yep. I've been known to do it."

The three men shared a hearty laugh as they headed toward Monique's house.

When the vehicle pulled into Monique's driveway, the door opened and out ran Neveah. Before the car fully stopped, she pulled on the back door where Art was sitting. He opened it from the inside and jumped into her arms.

"Are you okay? Did they hurt you in there?" she asked, rubbing his face and inspecting him from head to toe.

Art took Neveah in his arms, hugging her tightly. "I'm fine. Better now that I'm here with you."

Akadeus walked over to the pair and waved his arms over his head. "Hello! Father here. Do you care if I'm okay?" He laughed heartily when he was ignored. "I guess I'm on my own."

Art and Neveah separated as the group went into the home, where Monique stood with the baby in her arms. Seeing her aunt holding her daughter made Neveah smile. Maybe Monique would be sort of a stand-in grandmother until Wyleena was able to get out of jail. As long as Monique had a relationship of some sort with the girl, Neveah would be satisfied.

"Is anybody hungry? I fixed some spaghetti, salad, and garlic bread. I even made some Kool-Aid for you."

"My stomach is a little tense so I don't think I can eat right now, but I will in a little while," Art reported.

"I feel the same way," said Akadeus, taking the baby from Monique.

"Now that we've settled that, what did y'all do?" Monique asked with her hands on her hips. "I'm worried about you, Aaron."

"I need to know, too," Everette said as he took off his suit coat and got comfortable sitting on the couch. Monique maneuvered across the room and sat next to him.

Akadeus and Art looked at each other, then back at the other people in the room.

"We might as well tell everyone at the same time," Art explained, moving to a loveseat where Neveah sat as well.

Akadeus sat in a chair by the fireplace and prepared to speak.

"Years ago, Nasia and I ran into some financial difficulty. Things were really bad, to the point we literally thought we were going to have to live in our car and we weren't sure how we would be able to eat. Neither of us had any prospects for work and we were out of unemployment benefits." He paused and made eye contact with everyone around the room. "The worst happened and we ended up homeless. We met all of these other people, Art was one of them, who were living on the street.

Everybody wanted to get off the street but we didn't know how," Akadeus explained.

Art continued, "Someone suggested we get social security numbers and other information especially for people who were deceased. Once we got that information, we opened bank accounts and applied for credit cards, bought a bunch of equipment and stuff we could sell. We expanded to stealing their social security checks and their property if they didn't have any family. We built quite the enterprise and it allowed us all to get off the street."

"The problem was law enforcement found out about it somehow, but they only knew about Nasia for some reason. She took the rap for all of us and ended up doing time, letting us go free. When she was released, she was mad and threatened to have us all arrested for our involvement. That's when we started The Family of Saints and the guys who were working with us became husband-mates as a way to pay Nasia back for her sacrifice."

No one said a word. Everette stood and walked a few steps back and forth. Finally, he turned his attention to Akadeus. "How long ago did all of this take place? Before you answer, it's very important you are as accurate as possible."

"I'd say it was about eight years ago. Right, Art?"

"At least."

A wide smile formed on Everette's face.

"Art and Akadeus, you can relax. The statute of limitations has passed, meaning you can't be prosecuted for this crime. I'll take care of this right away."

CHAPTER 47

Art and Neveah were determined to spend some time alone just to talk and connect with one another. With caring for Artrice and trying to get their lives back on track, things had been moving nonstop since they'd left The Family of Saints. They took advantage of Artrice's napping to simply sit on Monique's patio and relax with each other.

They each got a beverage of their choice and met on the patio and let the breeze flow over them for a little while. Neveah felt there was peace in the quiet and loved the fact that she and Art were comfortable enough to sit in the silence together.

"This is nice, isn't it?" Art asked as he reached for Neveah's hand.

Neveah placed her hand in his and said, "I was just thinking that. We have a great friendship and I love that."

Art looked across the yard as he took a sip of his green tea. "Friendship?"

"Yes," Neveah said, noting the disappointment in Art's voice. "You don't agree?"

Art chuckled and responded, "So, does that mean we're just friends?"

"We're more than friends, Art."

"I'm confused. Let me ask you this. How would you feel if I started dating someone else?"

Neveah put her cup up to her mouth and took a couple of sips. Art was an awesome man and she knew he loved and cared about her. She definitely felt they were a great couple, but she hadn't considered how she would define the relationship before now.

"I wouldn't like it at all."

"What does that tell you?"

"Just because I wouldn't like it doesn't say anything about our relationship, right?"

"It says something about how you feel about me. I'm going to be completely honest with you. After all of that time in The Family of Saints I'm going for what I want and what I want is for you to be my wife. I love you, Neveah."

"I care about you, too."

"Care about me? Wow! Even after everything we've been through, you don't love me?"

"I didn't say that," Neveah said.

"What are you saying?"

Neveah didn't respond. She could hear the anger in Art's voice increase so she decided not to respond, letting things cool off for a moment. Instead, she sipped her beverage.

"Let me show you something," Art said, pulling a ring box from his pocket and opening it. "I was prepared to propose to you before we had this conversation."

Neveah drew in a breath. "It's beautiful," she said, reaching for the ring.

Art pulled it out of Neveah's reach. "This ring is for the woman I marry. Not a friend."

Art closed the ring box and went into the house, leaving Neveah to process what had happened.

A half-hour later, Neveah was still sitting on the patio looking off into the distance. Her thoughts were of Art and the conversation they'd had. Neveah's mind spun as she mulled over what was said as well as what wasn't said.

Art had obviously been a tremendous help and support to her. She knew that if she couldn't count on anyone else, she could count on him. He'd done so much for her including helping her find and visit her mother, protecting her in The Family of Saints, and even supporting her while she gave birth to her daughter. Though she'd probably never told him, her feelings for him went way beyond those of a friend. She loved him and didn't want to lose him. *Why couldn't she find it within herself to officially enter into the type of relationship Art wanted?* After all, the way she felt about Art was clear. There was no doubt about that.

Neveah heard the patio door open but no one said anything. She turned to see Monique standing there.

"I saw Art come in a little while ago. He seemed a little upset. I was trying to give you some space, but I thought I'd come out to see if you wanted to talk about it," Monique said, placing one foot outside.

Neveah waved her aunt over. She could use another point of view and she trusted Auntie Monique to give her the best advice she could. Even after their recent tiff, she believed the woman loved her and wanted the best for her.

"I think Art's going to leave me," Neveah started, her eyes welling up.

"Why do you think that?"

"He wants to marry me."

"That doesn't sound like someone who wants to leave."

"He's disappointed because I really hadn't thought about our relationship with so much other stuff going on. Apparently, he didn't appreciate that."

"Do you love him?"

"I think so."

"I think you do, too."

"Auntie Monique, I'm only eighteen, I'm a new mother, I really don't know what's going to happen beyond today. How can I get into a serious relationship right now?"

Monique leaned over and looked her niece in the eyes, "Baby girl, you already are in a serious relationship. I know you may feel a little unstable because of what you've been through, but don't be afraid to love him back."

Neveah thought about the truth of her aunt's advice. Maybe that was the problem...she was scared.

The patio door opened again and Art appeared. "I just wanted to grab my tea."

After getting his tea, he turned and moped back toward the house.

"Art, wait!"

Art turned and waited to hear what Neveah had to say.

"I love you and I don't want to lose you. I want to be your wife, but there's so much going on and I don't know if I'm really ready for it right now. I just need you to be patient with me." Neveah's heart sunk when Art didn't appear the least bit moved by her statement. "I just wanted you to know that," she whispered.

Several beats passed before Art approached Neveah, grabbed her face with both hands and placed a soft kiss on her lips, catching her completely off-guard. Neveah regained her composure and returned the kiss with a more passionate one.

"I'm so sorry I didn't hear what you were trying to tell me over the voice of my own desires. Please forgive me."

"I accept your apology. I didn't mean to upset you but I had to tell you the truth. Please don't leave."

As if on que, Artrice's cry blasted through the baby monitor outside with them.

"I guess we'd better break this up. The princess has awakened."

"I'll get her." Startled, Neveah and Art turned to find Monique still standing on the patio. "You two just sit out here and relax. I'll let you know if I need you." Monique went into the house leaving Neveah and Art to continue their conversation.

***

The position of Monique's house on the corner provided Neveah and Art a direct view of Akadeus as he nervously paced the sidewalk. The two wondered if he was losing it considering he appeared to be holding a passionate conversation with someone who wasn't there.

"What's going on with Akadeus?" Art wondered aloud. "He's been out there pacing for a while."

"I don't know but he seems pretty tense," Neveah headed toward her father. "I'm going to check on him."

As Neveah approached Akadeus, she saw a car pull up to the curb near him. He went to it once the window went down, revealing Nasia.

Nasia peeked around Akadeus, smiled and waved at Neveah. "How are you?" Nasia asked.

"I'm fine." Neveah walked closer to Akadeus. "What is she doing here?" she whispered. "She tried to send you and Art to jail."

"Listen, little girl, mind your own business." Nasia flicked her wrist at Neveah a few times as if to dismiss her.

Nasia looked past Neveah. She squinted before a smile crept across her face. "Is that you, Art? Come here and give me a hug," Nasia said, waving Art over while keeping her eyes focused on Neveah.

"Hi, Nasia. Good to see you," Art responded as he stood next to Neveah.

"Oh, I don't get a hug? Come on, you've known me much longer than you've known her." Nasia tilted her head and smirked at Neveah. "Are you that insecure? Are you scared you can't keep your man? Girl, you need to get that under control because that is not cute at all," Nasia said, moving her index finger from side to side with each syllable she spoke.

"Stop antagonizing her, Nasia," Akadeus warned his wife.

"I'll leave little Neveah alone." Nasia swiveled her head back to Akadeus. "I came here to talk to you anyway."

"Okay, I'm listening."

"After you all left, I had a lot of time to think. I realized I treated you and the other guys wrong. Especially you since you're my husband. I was extremely resentful because the whole time I was in prison, you never once came to see me."

"Nasia, I was afraid if I came, I would end up…"

"Right in prison too which is where you should've been since you committed the same crime I did. You put your own comfort and security ahead of me and that hurt. I was wrong for issuing my own form of punishment on you and for that, I do apologize."

"I apologize for how I handled that situation, too. If I had it to do over again, I would definitely do things differently."

"You know that is the first time you admitted you were wrong and I accept your apology. But we have another problem. You haven't been honest about who you really are and that's deceitful. On top of that, you abandoned me again when you all left The Family. All of that made me realize I can't trust you."

"I admit I've made some serious mistakes. All I can say is I'm sorry and I'm willing to do whatever is needed to show you just how sorry I am for what I've done."

"That's the thing, Akadeus. I'm sorry, too. Sorry I didn't divorce you when I got out of prison. But I won't take you back this time. It's over. I've filed for divorce and you'll be served shortly. I'm also disconnecting this cell phone so you'll only be able to contact me through my attorney."

"Please don't do this, Nasia. I'll do anything you want. Anything!" Akadeus fell to his knees, begging his wife not to end their relationship. "Please!"

"Goodbye, Akadeus," Nasia said as she put the car in gear and sped away, leaving Akadeus sobbing at the curb.

Neveah walked over to her dad and knelt next to him. "Come on. Let's go inside."

Akadeus responded by laying out on the ground.

"Art, can you help me," she asked, standing and attempting to pull Akadeus up.

Art came over and lifted his friend up. The still-sobbing Akadeus stood under his own power, with his arms over the shoulders of his daughter and friend, and allowed himself to be led into his sister's home. Monique followed and closed the door behind them.

CHAPTER 48

Two weeks later, the group piled into Monique's SUV and headed toward the Michigan state line. The excitement in the vehicle was electric. The purpose for this trip made it that way. There was also a little nervousness considering it wasn't clear where things would go in the future for any of those involved.

Neveah peeked at Artrice then at Art. She loved her little family, though she and Art weren't officially a couple yet. True to his word, he hadn't pushed Neveah but instead let her move at her own pace concerning their relationship. Over the past several months Art had proven to be dedicated to her and once she was born, Artrice as well. He had even gotten a job at a local factory to insure he could contribute while they lived at Monique's house and when he and Neveah got married, that he could take care of the family as well. There was nothing holding Neveah back from moving forward in their relationship with this man except her. She was the reason the two weren't married and living their own "happily ever after." However, if she wasn't ready, she just wasn't ready. Her hope was that Art wouldn't tire of waiting for her but that he would continue to be a steadying force in both her and Artrice's lives.

Neveah's eyes fell on the prison where her mother had been held for the past year. Though she never complained, Neveah knew her mother had struggled significantly being locked up in this place. While it was true Wyleena had committed a crime, she had done so to protect her daughter against a sexual predator named Otis. During their phone conversations, Wyleena had often expressed regret over falling in love with a man who seemed to be the father figure her daughter so desperately desired, but who was obviously setting her up to satisfy his sexual desires as well. Wyleena had to grieve the loss of her dream, the affect the abuse had on her daughter, and the time she was missing from her family.

Today was an important day as Wyleena was meeting her grandchild for the first time. The anticipated visit was finally happening and Akadeus and Art had been added to the visitor list as well.

The group parked and then entered the lobby, checked in and were eventually led into a room with a number of couches and chairs scattered around the space for their visit. The attendant directed everyone to where they should sit. Shortly afterward, Wyleena entered the waiting area. When she laid eyes on Akadeus, she smiled at him and he returned the favor. Neveah was surprised at the mutual admiration in their eyes. If she didn't know better, she would say they still had feelings for each other.

"Hello everyone," Wyleena said, approaching her visitors.

When she got to Akadeus, she paused and looked him in the eyes. "Aaron, it's so good to see you. You're looking good."

"Though I wish it was under different circumstances, I'm glad to see you, too. You're still fine as ever," he said, allowing his eyes to linger on hers.

"Why thank you," Wyleena responded, running her hand over her salt and pepper hair.

She moved to Art next. "You must be Art."

"I am, Miss Wyleena. I'm happy to meet you."

Wyleena stared at him for a few moments. "Neveah, I can tell he's genuine and he's cute. Anybody ever say you look like Blake Griffin?"

"A time or two." Art laughed and the rest of the group joined in.

Finally, she approached her daughter and granddaughter. She shared the biggest smile for them. Wyleena's eyes landed on her granddaughter who was sleeping in her mother's arms. She smiled as she ran her finger down the side of the baby's face, causing Artrice to turn her head towards it, searching for a bottle. The guard pointed toward the empty seat next to Neveah and they both sat.

"She's beautiful just like you were when you were this age."

"Do you want to hold her?" Neveah asked, positioning the child to be passed to her grandmother.

"Can I?" Wyleena asked a guard standing nearby who nodded affirmatively.

With the baby cradled in her arms, Wyleena rocked her and hummed a song. The baby looked into her grandmother's eyes and appeared to be listening. The exchange was going well until the baby whimpered.

Neveah took the covering off of a bottle and offered it to her mother. "She might be hungry."

Wyleena offered the bottle to Artrice, who greedily attacked it.

"How are you, baby?" Wyleena asked Neveah. "You look wonderful."

"I'm fine, Mama. I'm happy to see you. Glad you finally get to meet Artrice."

"Me, too. I'm so sorry I got myself into this mess but I just lost it when I saw what Otis was doing to you. I should've handled it differently then I would've been able to help you with this beautiful baby girl."

"I know, Mama. We'll get through this. Besides, I have Akadeus and Art to help me."

Wyleena's gaze fell on the two men sitting across from she and her daughter.

"Aaron I've been wondering what is going on with this Akadeus stuff? Where did that come from?"

"I did some stuff as Aaron that I'm ashamed of so I changed my name to create a new identity for myself. I went in search of a strong name and came up with Akadeus."

Wyleena nodded. "I think I can understand that. I heard you were married. Where's your wife?"

Akadeus dropped his head. "She left me."

"I'm sorry to hear that. Maybe she'll change her mind."

"Thank you and I hope she does."

Wyleena removed the empty bottle from the sleeping Artrice's mouth and handed it to her mother. She carefully put the infant on her shoulder and patted her back to burp her. After a couple of burps, Wyleena cradled her again as the baby slept.

"Art, it's really good to finally meet you. I've heard a lot about you."

"It's great to finally meet you, too."

"Neveah told me how helpful you've been to her and Artrice. I'm so thankful she has someone to help her until I get out and can help."

"I care about these two young ladies and I'm glad I can help."

"Hmmm. I can see that. What are your intentions for my daughter?"

"Mama!" Neveah said, trying to stop her mother's questioning of Art. She and her mother had spoken about her relationship with Art on a number of occasions so she didn't understand why she would push Art.

"It's okay, Neveah. I don't have a problem answering questions from the mother of the woman I'm going to marry one day."

"Marriage?" Wyleena asked. "Are you two engaged? she asked as she craned her neck, looking at Neveah's left hand.

"Not yet. She's not ready," Art mentioned. "I'm willing to wait because I know she is so worth it. I've already asked Akadeus but haven't had a chance to ask you. Will you allow me to ask for your daughter's hand in marriage? I know she's going to say yes one day, so I thought I'd ask you ahead of time. Don't want any delays, you know."

"I knew before I met you that you were an honorable man and you love my daughter and granddaughter. You're the perfect man for them. I give you my blessing to get married whenever you two decide." Wyleena stared at Neveah for a few moments, causing her daughter to squirm. "Ask her now, Art. I think you might get the answer you desire."

Neveah's jaw dropped. *Why would her mother do that?*

"You think so?" Art asked, focusing on Neveah.

"Try it and let's see what happens," Wyleena suggested.

Art crossed the small space separating him and Neveah, then knelt on one knee in front of her. He took her hand and gazed into her eyes.

"Neveah, I'm going to keep this simple. Will you marry me?" he asked, never breaking eye contact with her.

Neveah's eyes and nose leaked as she pondered what Art was asking. She realized she had fallen in love with him long ago, but had been afraid to allow herself to reciprocate that love for various reasons. In this moment, she knew her fears were unfounded and she knew what her answer would be. She looked at her parents and her baby who was still resting in her grandmother's arms, then turned her attention back to Art.

"I know I told you I wasn't sure I was ready to get married and I appreciate your willingness to give me time. I've been thinking about us and I'm ready to agree to be your wife. No question. I love you too, Art."

Art's eyes bulged and his mouth gaped open.

"Are you saying yes?" he asked.

Neveah nodded her head as the flow of her tears increased. Art stood and lifted her into a huge bear hug as applause broke out in the visitor's room.

The security staff quieted the crowd, directing everyone to resume their visit with the prisoner they were originally there to visit. Art was asked to return to his seat which he reluctantly did.

Wyleena smiled and spoke to Art. "I told you." Then to her daughter, she said, "I'm happy for you. You have a good man."

She returned her attention to Art and said, "Take good care of my babies. I'll be getting out of here one day. Don't let me have to come find you." She playfully pointed at Art.

"Don't worry, Wyleena. I'll keep my eyes on things until you get out," Akadeus said as his eyes turned blue.

"Neither of you have anything to worry about. I've been waiting for a woman like Neveah and I intend to treat her and Artrice like the queen and princess they are. They'll want for nothing. That's my promise."

Neveah smiled at her fiancé. When Art first introduced her to the idea of God's love, she hadn't believed it was possible considering all she'd been through. Now God had outdone Himself by loving her enough to send this perfect man into her life to love and care for her and her daughter. Neveah looked at the father she thought was dead and realized even his intentional absence was a sign of his love for her. Wyleena showed the ultimate love for Neveah and was paying the price for her actions.

Now Neveah knew that God and His love were real regardless of what she encountered in her life. She no longer had to wonder what God's name was...she knew it was love.

Dear Reader,

Thank you so much for reading Neveah's story in *What is God's Name*. I hope you enjoyed it. My desire is that you take away a message that will have a positive impact on your life. If I achieve that goal, I did my job. I know there are millions of other books you could spend your time reading. I am honored you chose to read one of mine.

If you liked *What is God's Name*, please consider writing a review on the online retailer website of your choice. Also, visit me at my website, www.DarlissBatchelor.com. There, you'll learn about my other books, read excerpts, see videos and much more. You will also have the opportunity to sign up for updates, giving you access to exclusive content, early release information, discounts and freebies.

Until the next book,

Darliss Batchelor

P.S. You can also find me on the web:
Website: www.DarlissBatchelor.com
Facebook: www.FaceBook.com/BooksByDarliss
Amazon Author Page: www.amazon.com/author/DarlissBatchelor
Goodreads: www.Goodreads.com/DarlissBatchelor

Chapter 1

Chriselle labored up the stairs. She walked past a few empty bedrooms and a full bathroom to the last room on the left. It was her daughter Leslie's bedroom. She entered the room with its soft orange sorbet colored walls, wood floors, white bedroom furniture and orange and fuchsia floral comforter. Sitting in the cantaloupe-colored chair near the window, Chriselle began to think about Leslie and Bryce's wedding earlier that day.

"I now pronounce you man and wife. You may kiss the bride."

Chriselle reminisced about her daughter's wedding while pulling a tissue from the box sitting on the side table. Those words were life changing. They changed Chriselle's life when she said them over thirty years ago, and they changed her child's life today. Her last child, Leslie, was now officially someone's wife, complete with a change of address form and a moving van.

Chriselle remembered all those years ago when she said those same vows. She had dreams and thoughts about what her life would be like as a Mrs. She just didn't know how big those dreams were at the time.

The look of love in the eyes of Leslie and her new husband, Bryce, said it all. Their deep love and commitment was evident today. No one and nothing in the world could come between them today. Their minds couldn't even comprehend that anything in life could be better. However, sometimes things indeed change and you find out that "forever" means something much shorter.

The traditional wedding vows include a promise to stay together until death. Chriselle wondered if anything other than physical death counted. She felt like she died as a person, as a woman. All those years of raising children, taking care of a house, and over thirty years of being a wife caused her to forget what her life was like beforehand.

Gazing out of the nearby window overlooking the family's swimming pool, Chriselle realized Leslie wouldn't be home making blueberry pancakes for breakfast tomorrow morning. She wouldn't be sitting with Chriselle in the adult Sunday school class as she'd been doing since she became old enough to join her. Instead, she'd be in some exotic location enjoying her first days of marriage not even thinking about the fact Chriselle felt lost.

Chriselle moved to the bed and stretched her body across it, inhaling the residual signature scent of her youngest daughter. Her thoughts shifted to the nights she sat in this bed with Leslie and read Bible stories. She recalled kneeling on this very floor with her to pray. The memory of Leslie announcing her engagement came to mind. That was when Chriselle felt she'd lost her purpose.

All of her children— three sons and two daughters—had gone

on with their lives. How dare they do that? They must have forgotten everything she'd done for them. She wiped runny noses, spent more time in the emergency room than she cared to remember, attempted to mend broken hearts, kept them clean and presentable, and introduced them to Jesus Christ. And what did she get in return? She got an empty house. And she found herself resentful of it. Yes, they often came to visit and brought their spouses and children. Still, Chriselle was overcome by emotional and physical emptiness.

Drew, Chriselle's husband, came into the room just as she crushed her tissue and added it to the pile already established on the bed. She didn't want him to see her like this. She didn't want him to know about her pain. After looking into his eyes, she realized he already knew this pain almost as intimately as she did. He held her in his arms and stroked her hair, his best effort at comforting her. She didn't think he could feel it as deeply as she did. He had a life. She'd been a housewife and mother all these years. Now that the demands were different, Chriselle didn't know what to do with herself.

Surrounded by Drew's arms, Chriselle couldn't remember the last time she felt the spark she and Drew once shared. She realized she didn't even feel a tingle. What happened to me? What happened to us?

Other books by Darliss Batchelor

Secrets

Hell is a Skyscraper: A Trio of Novelettes

Something Else to Want

The Make-Believe Wives

The Make-Believe Family

Edgar's Embrace (limited edition e-book)

Available at www.DarlissBatchelor.com